LITTLE LEAGUE®
STATE SHOW-DOWN

LITTLE LEAGUE®
STATE
SHOW-
DOWN

MATT CHRISTOPHER

Ⓛ Ⓑ
Little, Brown and Company
New York Boston

Copyright © 2013 by Matt Christopher Royalties, Inc.

Little, Brown and Company

Hachette Book Group
237 Park Avenue, New York, NY 10017
Visit our website at www.lb-kids.com
www.mattchristopher.com

Little, Brown and Company is a division of Hachette Book Group, Inc.
The Little, Brown name and logo are trademarks of Hachette Book Group, Inc.

The publisher is not responsible for websites (or their content)
that are not owned by the publisher.

First Edition: October 2013

Matt Christopher® is a registered trademark of Matt Christopher Royalties, Inc.

Little League Baseball, Little League, the medallion and the keystone
are registered trademarks and service marks belonging exclusively to
Little League Baseball, Incorporated.

© 2013 Little League Baseball, Incorporated. All Rights Reserved.

Text written by Stephanie True Peters

Library of Congress Cataloging-in-Publication Data
Christopher, Matt.
State showdown / Matt Christopher. — First edition.
    pages cm. — (Little League ; 3)
    Summary: Eleven-year-old cousins Carter Jones and Liam McGrath must both deal with grudges that threaten to break apart their All-Star teams during post-season play.
    ISBN 978-0-316-22044-6 (hardback) — ISBN 978-0-316-24844-0 (ebook)
[1. Baseball—Fiction. 2. Cousins—Fiction. 3. Interpersonal relations—Fiction.] I. Title.
PZ7.C458Ssm 2013
[Fic]—dc23
                                    2013015030

10   9   8   7   6   5   4   3   2   1

RRD-C

Printed in the United States of America

The Little League® Pledge

I trust in God

I love my country

And will respect its laws

I will play fair

And strive to win

But win or lose

I will always do my best

CHAPTER
ONE

Whizz! Swish! Thud!

"Stee-rike two!" The home plate umpire made a fist in the air.

Liam McGrath, twelve-year-old catcher for the Ravenna All-Star team, plucked the baseball from his mitt and threw it back to pitcher Phillip DiMaggio. He licked his lips, tasting the dust that coated them.

"Okay, DiMaggio," he said under his breath. "Let's finish this now."

It was the early evening, top of the fifth inning of the final District tournament game, and the temperature was hovering in the mideighties. Liam was sweating buckets beneath his padded gear and mask. He wiped his damp palm on his pant leg before settling back into his crouch.

The Orchard City batter must have been feeling the heat, too. He mopped his face with the sleeve of his Little League uniform and then resumed his stance in the box.

Orchard City was up by one. It had two outs but also had runners on first and third. One good hit could sweeten its lead.

Liam had no intention of letting that happen. Too much was on the line. The winners of today's game would advance to the Sectional tournament, putting them one step closer to the ultimate youth baseball competition: the Little League Baseball World Series. The losing team would go home, its postseason run at an end. Liam had worked too hard, overcome too many challenges this season, to pack away his gear—and his World Series dreams—after this game.

At the top of his list of challenges was the boy standing on the mound. Liam and Phillip had a long-standing rivalry that dated back to the previous World Series. They'd been on opposing sides then, and battling for the U.S. Championship. Phillip's team won when he struck out Liam in spectacular—and, for Liam, mortifying—fashion.

If anyone had told Liam that one day he'd be Phillip's catcher, he would have said pigs would fly first. And yet here he was, readying himself for DiMaggio's next pitch.

But only because Owen got food poisoning, he reminded himself. Teammate Owen Berg had been slotted to catch. But before the second of a doubleheader, he got violently sick to his stomach.

So the catcher's job fell to Liam. Before the game, he and Phillip agreed to put their past differences aside. They'd stuck to their agreement—sort of.

After Ravenna's first inning in the field, Phillip told Liam there was a problem. "I can't see your signals. Your leg is hiding your fingers. Maybe you could try widening your stance?"

Liam shook his head. "Any wider, and the first-base coach might see the signals, figure out what they mean, and tell the batter."

Phillip gave him a skeptical look. "Are you kidding me?"

"It could happen," Liam said defensively.

Phillip frowned. "Listen, if this"—he bounced a finger in the air between them—"is going to work, you have to listen to me."

The two locked eyes. Tension crackled between them.

Liam looked away first. Few things, he knew, sent a team off course faster than friction between pitcher and catcher. He also knew that a big part of the catcher's job was putting the pitcher at ease. If doing what Phillip asked helped them win the game, then he'd do it.

As it turned out, widening his stance was just one adjustment Phillip asked him to make.

"Can you move your mitt into position sooner? It throws off my timing if I have to wait for the target."

"You're pretty noisy behind that plate. How about a little less chatter after an out?"

"Owen held his throwing hand behind his knee, not his back. Maybe you should try that."

Liam did everything Phillip suggested without complaint. But his temper was rising.

Now they were one strike away from ending Orchard City's scoring threat. Liam flashed the signal for a changeup. Phillip nodded, wiped his face on his right shoulder, and then wound up and unleashed the off-speed pitch. The batter started to swing but then stopped.

Thud!

To Liam's eye, the ball had just missed the strike zone. So when he made the catch, he twitched his glove a fraction of an inch toward the center. He held his breath, hoping the umpire would think he had caught the ball in the zone.

The official hesitated. Then he made the call. "Ball!"

"Good eye, good eye!" the batter's teammates yelled.

On the mound, Phillip's mouth tightened. He nodded curtly when Liam signaled for another changeup, gave his face another swipe on his shoulder, and then sent the ball on its way. This time, its slow speed fooled the batter into swinging too early.

"Strike three!"

Fans for Ravenna and Orchard City applauded as the teams switched sides. In the dugout, Liam grabbed his water bottle and sighed with contentment as the cool water soothed his parched throat.

Then Phillip dropped down next to him and his contentment fizzled. *Now what?* he thought.

"You moved your glove too much on that catch," Phillip said.

Liam couldn't let that one go by. "Excuse me?"

"That first changeup? If you hadn't jerked your mitt when you caught it, the ump would have called it a strike."

Liam bristled. "He would have called it a ball, because that's what it was."

"Oh, yeah? Well, I say it could have gone either way."

Liam was about to tell Phillip he was dead wrong when he noticed a few of their teammates watching them. So he bit back his words and turned his attention to the game.

Second baseman Matt Finch had singled. Now slugger Rodney Driscoll was up. He let the first pitch go by but took a big cut at the second.

Crack!

The Ravenna players and fans leaped to their feet. The ball soared over the outfield fence—a two-run homer! Ravenna had the lead!

The team looked good to add even more to its side of the scoreboard when Phillip and Liam singled one after the other.

Then Orchard City changed pitchers and the new hurler got the next three batters out in order. When Orchard City's own hitters tried to erase Ravenna's lead, however, Liam and his teammates denied them. Final score: Ravenna 3, Orchard City 2.

The boys filed quickly through the "good game" hand-slap. Afterward, all the players received a special trading pin to commemorate their participation in the District tournament. Then the Ravenna teammates gathered for a photo with the District Champs banner.

Finally, they headed to the dugout for a postgame team meeting.

Up until that moment, the boys had held their happiness in check so as not to add to Orchard City's disappointment. But now they broke out in cheers.

"We're going to Sectionals!" Rodney whooped loudest of all.

Just then, Rodney's brother, Sean, ran over with his father's cell phone. "Call for you, Dad," he said breathlessly. "It's Owen's mom."

Dr. Driscoll was the team manager and Rodney and Sean's father. He took the phone from Sean and had a brief conversation. When he hung up, his expression was grim.

"Owen didn't have food poisoning. His appendix ruptured. He's had an operation and will be fine, but he's sidelined for the season."

Liam's heart started beating faster. *If Owen's out, does that mean . . . I'm in? And if I'm in*—his gaze flicked to Phillip—*is that good or bad?*

CHAPTER
TWO

Carter Jones tossed a pink rubber ball from hand to hand.

"So, doofus, what's your big news, other than your team is going to Sectionals, too?"

Carter was in his bedroom, video-chatting with Liam. Cousins and best friends, they used to hang out together all the time. They used to play baseball together, too, with Liam behind the plate and Carter, a top-notch southpaw, on the mound.

Then last winter, Liam and his family moved from Pennsylvania to Southern California. Now the boys caught up through texting, phone calls, and video-chats.

Baseball was the main topic of many conversations—especially now that both of their teams were heading to Sectionals.

"I might be Phillip's catcher from now on," Liam said.

The ball dropped from Carter's hand and rolled under his bunk beds.

Liam had had his trouble with DiMaggio, but so had Carter. Two summers back, Phillip played a practical joke on him during Little League Baseball Camp. At the end of the session, Carter had left bearing a huge grudge against the California pitcher. The idea that his cousin might be catching for Phillip left him cold. He felt even more uneasy about it when Liam told him about Phillip's "corrections."

"Are you kidding me?" he fumed. "Who does he think he is?"

A sharp knock on the bedroom door cut into their conversation. Carter twisted around in his desk chair. "I wonder who that could be."

"Only one way to find out," Liam said.

"Open the door?" Carter guessed.

"No," Liam said, and then bellowed, "Get in here, quick! I need help!"

The door banged open. A blond-haired boy about Carter's height rushed in. "What's wrong?" he cried, his brown eyes darting around wildly.

Liam laughed. "Is that Jerry? Or Charlie? Tell him to get in camera range so I can say hi!"

Jerry Tuckerman and Charlie Murray had played on the Forest Park All-Star team last year with Carter and Liam. But the blond boy wasn't Jerry or Charlie. His name was Ash LaBrie. Liam had never met him—not officially, that is, although he certainly knew who Ash was.

Ash had moved into Liam's old house with his mother last winter. He was the same age as the cousins and, like them, played baseball. This past season, he'd taken over Liam's spot as Carter's catcher.

While no one could ever replace Liam as his favorite catcher, Carter couldn't deny that he and Ash made a good pair. He believed Liam accepted that fact. Still, he couldn't help squirming inside when Ash moved into Liam's view.

Ash spoke first. "So you're Liam. Nice to finally meet you."

"Yeah." Liam's voice was cool. "And you're Ashley."

"Liam," Carter broke in hurriedly, "I told you he

goes by Ash. He's just kidding around," he added to Ash. "He does that."

"Oh, right." Ash looked back at Liam. "Congrats on getting on the All-Star team after all. Too bad you're not catching, but outfield is important, too."

Liam's eyes narrowed. "As a matter of fact," he said tersely, "I could be starting at catcher in Sectionals."

"Really?" Ash raised his eyebrows. "No offense, but what are your coaches thinking switching things around like that in the postseason?" He turned to Carter. "I mean, wouldn't it be hard for you if Coach Harrison replaced me as your catcher now?"

Carter bit his lip. Ash was right; it would be a big adjustment for him to make. But he felt caught in the middle. Agreeing with Ash would make it seem as if he thought Liam's playing catcher would be a liability for his team. So he just shrugged.

Ash seemed satisfied with that. "By the way, Liam, what do you think about Carter's killer pitch? Pretty tough to get a glove on it, isn't it?"

Now Carter squirmed even more. His "killer pitch" was a knuckleball, a pitch that practically bounced through the air as it approached the plate. The movement fooled batters but was also tough for catchers to follow.

Ash had learned to handle it after lots of practice. But last month, when Carter had paid a surprise visit to the McGraths, Liam had bobbled every knuckleball he'd thrown.

Carter hadn't told Ash about that, of course. But the look on Liam's face made it clear he thought Ash was making fun of him.

"No offense, *Ash*"—Liam repeated Ash's own words and emphasized the name with sarcasm—"but Carter and I were having a private conversation here. So . . ." He circled his hand in an impatient, tell-us-what-you-want-already gesture.

Ash blinked. "Oh, right. Carter, your mother sent me up to get you. She's in the kitchen with my mom."

"Okay. Liam, I guess I better go." Carter held his fist up to the screen. "Sectionals, man."

Liam glanced at Ash but then raised his fist, too. "Sectionals." Together they bumped the screen three times. Then Liam signed off.

"What was that?" Ash asked, imitating the fist-bump gesture.

Carter shrugged. "Just our way of wishing each other good luck. Come on. Let's go see what our moms want."

Mrs. Jones, a petite brunette with light brown eyes,

was pouring herbal tea for Mrs. LaBrie when the boys entered the kitchen.

"Hi, Carter," Mrs. LaBrie greeted. Blond like her son with an athletic build and shrewd blue eyes, she had a slight southern accent that always reminded Carter of a Civil War movie he'd once seen. She took a sip of tea before explaining the reason for the visit. "I'm here to tell you that I had asked your mom for a favor. It seems the person I'd hired to run the Diamond Champs summer programs can't take the job after all."

The Diamond Champs was an indoor baseball facility with state-of-the-art pitching tunnels, batting cages, a full turf infield, and much more. Carter and his friends practically lived there on rainy days.

"I can run the programs myself, of course," Mrs. LaBrie continued. "But that means I can't go to Sectionals."

"So Ash will be staying with us instead," Carter's mother said.

The upcoming tournament was in a town that was three hours away by car. Carter, like most of the players, was staying with his parents at a nearby hotel. Ash and his mother were booked at the same place.

"We've changed the reservation to two adjoining

rooms," Mrs. LaBrie said. "You boys can stay in one and Carter's parents in the other."

"And Mrs. LaBrie will take care of Lucky Boy while we're gone," Mrs. Jones put in, referring to Carter's small black-and-tan dog. "So everything's worked out just fine."

"I guess so," Carter replied. Deep down, though, he felt a prickle of apprehension.

Ash could be pretty intense when it came to baseball. Assuming Forest Park advanced to the final game of the tournament, they'd be together for at least three days, maybe four. What would it be like spending every minute of that time—meals, games, practices, free time, bedtime—with someone that intense?

CHAPTER
THREE

"Don't say another word until I get the camera rolling!" Melanie McGrath exclaimed.

Liam put his head in his hands and groaned as his sister ran from the kitchen. *Well, that was a huge mistake!* he thought.

It was Thursday morning, the day after the District win. Liam and Melanie had been having breakfast when Liam mentioned he might be catching for Phillip.

I should have known better, he thought. *To her, my problem is just another scene for her movie.*

A dark-haired, attractive sixteen-year-old, Melanie was an aspiring actress. Since the move to California, she had attended a private high school that specialized in theater, movies, and television. As a summer assignment, she was making a documentary of Liam's All-Star team. The movie would include clips of postseason games and practices as well as profiles of the coaches and players. But its real focus was Liam and Phillip's "former rivals, now teammates" story. The merest hint of a new angle to that story sent Melanie running for her camera.

Melanie returned a moment later, video camera on and aimed at Liam.

"Liam McGrath," she said, moving slowly toward him, "it's been less than a year since pitcher Phillip DiMaggio struck you out at the World Series. Now, unbelievably, you two may be paired up as pitcher and catcher in the next tournament. Can you tell me how you feel about that?"

"Oh, sure. Just a sec." Liam picked up a bagel and ripped out a large chunk with his teeth. Mouth full, he began gesturing grandly and talking while chewing. "Mumghph mrphth sphythathm. Mthmph."

Melanie put the camera down. "Funny," she said sarcastically. "Keep it up and I'll post the clip online."

Luckily, the arrival of Sean and Rodney stopped the argument before it escalated any further.

"Bagels, awesome!" Sean enthused as he stuck a garlic one in the toaster and pushed down the lever. "I was hoping for a second breakfast before practice."

Sean and Rodney were Liam's best friends in California. They had been adopted years earlier by Dr. Driscoll. By weird coincidence, they shared the exact same birthday. They liked to joke that they were twins, although anyone could see they weren't. Rodney was tall and lanky with tight dark curls, deep brown eyes, and chocolate-colored skin. Sean was slightly pudgy and a little on the short side, like Liam, and had fair, freckled skin, reddish hair, and blue eyes. Rodney was the better athlete of the two and had been selected for the Ravenna All-Stars. Sean hadn't expected to make the squad, so he wasn't disappointed when his name wasn't on the roster. If his loud cheers during games were any indication, he was his brother's biggest fan.

Garlic fumes from Sean's toasted bagel sent Melanie heading for the kitchen door. "I'll get my interview later," she said before she disappeared.

"What was that all about?" Rodney asked as he spread cream cheese on half a cinnamon-raisin bagel.

Liam sighed. "I was stupid enough to tell her I might be catching for Phillip."

"No *might* about it," Sean said absentmindedly. "Dad has you two paired up for the third Sectional game."

Rodney whacked his brother in the back of the head. "Dude, you weren't supposed to say anything!"

Sean looked guilty. "Whoops." Then he cheered up. "Well, he was going to find out this morning anyway. So, got any peanut butter?"

Liam fetched the jar from the pantry, too distracted by the news to consider how disgusting it was that Sean put peanut butter on a garlic bagel. "You're sure it's me, and not Cole?"

Rodney nodded. "Dad told us this morning. We swore we wouldn't tell." He whacked Sean again. "Promise breaker."

"Ow!" Sean rubbed his head and scowled. "Brother hitter."

"Guys," Liam interjected, glancing at the clock, "we're due at the field in twenty minutes."

With the first game of Sectionals approaching, Coach Driscoll had called for a light practice that morning. Rodney and Sean had biked to Liam's house. Now all three rode to the field. Liam and Rodney had backpacks with gloves, water, and cleats. Sean wasn't playing, but, as he said, "there are worse places to spend a morning than at the ball field."

Dr. Driscoll was already there. He took one look

at Sean's shifty expression and sighed. "You told him, didn't you?"

Sean hung his head. "Sorry, it just sort of slipped out."

His father drew a circle in the air with his finger. "Three laps around the outfield for breaking your promise."

Liam grinned as father and son took off. When he'd first met the coach, he hadn't been very impressed. With thinning hair, Harry Potter–style glasses, and a doughy physique, Dr. Driscoll had fumbled his way through the Little League tryouts in January. Sean and Rodney insisted that their father knew the game of baseball inside and out and that even if he couldn't play well, he would make a great team manager. Still, Liam had had his doubts.

It turned out Rodney and Sean were right. Dr. Driscoll had a knack for getting the most out of his players. Their team, the Pythons, had roared through the regular season with just two losses. They'd finished the District tournament undefeated. .

Meanwhile, Coach Driscoll had undergone a transformation. He'd started working out, so now his T-shirts no longer strained against his stomach. He'd upgraded his glasses to more fashionable frames. His hair would always be thin, but who could tell under his baseball cap?

After the three laps, Coach Driscoll summoned Liam to his side. "So, as Sean said, you'll be stepping in for Owen." He cocked his head to the side. "You got the position because things looked pretty solid between you and Phillip yesterday. Did I read that right?"

The question was asking about more than the previous day's game. Dr. Driscoll knew all about Liam's past problem with Phillip. He knew, too, that that problem had caused Liam to make some poor decisions during the regular season.

Liam had been convinced that players in his new Little League recognized him as the boy Phillip struck out during the World Series. Determined to erase the memory of that strikeout from their minds, he'd set his sights on becoming the top home run hitter in the league. He had success at the plate, but it came with a hefty price. His selfish goal turned him into a selfish player—and had cost him an All-Star spot. He was on the Ravenna roster now only because another boy withdrew before the season started.

Now, with Owen sidelined, he'd been given another unexpected chance, this time to play his favorite position. How would it sound if he turned around and complained about Phillip's corrections?

It'd sound as if I think my needs are more important than his, he thought. *In other words: selfish.*

"You read it right, sir," he finally said. "Phillip and I have buried the hatchet. You don't need to worry about us anymore."

CHAPTER FOUR

Arriving at destination," the computerized female voice of the Joneses' GPS announced.

"Thanks for stating the obvious," Mr. Jones said as he pulled into the hotel parking lot.

It was midmorning on Saturday, the first day of the Sectional tournament. Carter's team, Forest Park, was scheduled to play in the late afternoon. First, though, there was a welcome luncheon at the hotel for all the players, coaches, and family members. The Joneses had picked up Ash bright and early and arrived with time to spare.

Mr. Jones went inside to see if their rooms were ready. Carter got out and stretched. The acrid smell of hot blacktop practically curled his nostril hairs, but he didn't care. For the past three hours, Ash had been sharing details about Calder, the team they were facing later that day. That information was kept in a special binder along with notes about other teams in the Sectional tourney. Carter appreciated the lowdown, but now he needed a break.

Ash and Mrs. Jones got out, too. "Phew! The weather folks were right," Carter's mother said, fanning herself with a magazine. "The air is so thick with humidity you can practically cut it with a knife. So, you boys excited?"

"Excited, and a little nervous," Carter admitted.

"I just want to get started," Ash said.

The hotel's revolving glass doors deposited Mr. Jones back outside. "We're all set," he called.

The cool air enveloped them as they walked through the hotel lobby. They were by the elevator when Forest Park's manager, Mr. Harrison, happened by. An energetic man with thick black hair, beefy arms, and a snub nose, he had been Carter's Little League coach for the past two seasons and for last year's postseason. He shook hands with Mr. Jones and offered to take Mrs. Jones's bag. She waved him off with a smile of thanks.

"I'll see you all at the luncheon, then," the coach said, nodding as the foursome stepped into the elevator.

Their rooms were on the top floor, which was perfect, Mrs. Jones told them, because it meant there wouldn't be the sounds of people walking around above to bother them.

"I brought earplugs for everyone," she added, "in case there are any loud parties going on."

"And your white-noise machine to cancel out other annoying sounds?" Mr. Jones said, his eyes twinkling with mischief.

Carter's mother colored. "As a matter of fact, yes."

"My mom gets a little crazy if she's woken up in the middle of the night," Carter stage-whispered to Ash.

Mrs. Jones laughed. "I like my beauty sleep!"

Her husband put his arm around her and gave her a kiss. "You're beautiful enough without it."

Carter pretended to gag. But Ash didn't see. He was looking at Carter's parents with a wistful expression.

Carter didn't have any brothers or sisters, but he did have both his parents; Ash had only his mother. Carter didn't know anything about Ash's father because he'd never asked. He didn't want Ash to think he was prying. But he sometimes wondered about him.

The elevator doors opened on their floor. Their footsteps were hushed as they made their way down the long carpeted hallway to their adjoining rooms.

"Sweet," Carter said, taking in the two double beds and flat-screen television. He opened the drapes. Sliding glass doors led to a tiny balcony that overlooked a huge outdoor pool. "Check it out! That's Craig and Allen swimming down there."

Craig Ruckel played right field for Forest Park. Allen Avery was one of the team's shortstops.

Carter cupped his hands around his mouth and called down to them. They didn't look up.

"They must have some of Mom's earplugs in," Carter joked when Ash came out onto the balcony. "Hey, you want to go join them?"

Ash looked over his shoulder at the digital clock between their beds. "The lunch starts in fifteen minutes."

Carter was disappointed but saw that Craig and Allen were out of the pool and drying off anyway. "Oh well," he said. "We can go afterward, right?"

Ash frowned. "We could, but we shouldn't. You're pitching today, remember? You don't want to tire out your arm swimming. Save the pool for after we win."

Carter suppressed a sigh. Ash was probably right, but it was so hot out and the pool looked so inviting.

Liam would go in, he thought with just a tiny bit of bitterness.

Carter's mother poked her head through the

adjoining door then and told them it was time to head downstairs.

The luncheon took place in the hotel's dining room. Breakfast had been hours earlier and Carter's stomach growled when he saw the food. He filled his plate and then looked around for the other Forest Park players.

"Carter, Ash, over here!" Charlie called from a corner table. The rest of the team was there, too. Carter's parents sat with the other adults, leaving the boys to themselves.

Carter took a seat and examined his roast beef sandwich. Meat, American cheese, mayo, and lettuce on a bulky roll, no weird stuff like sun-dried tomato spread or horseradish sauce—just the way he liked it. He had just taken a big bite when Craig nudged him and pointed to a girl with long hair tied back into a ponytail.

"Look, Jones, it's your girlfriend."

Carter nearly choked on his sandwich.

Rachel Warburton had played on the Hawks, his regular-season Little League team. Funny, smart, confident, and with a powerful throwing arm, she reminded Carter of Liam. He liked her a lot, but just as a friend, not as a girlfriend. He was sure she felt the same way.

Rachel wove her way through the dining room. "Surprised to see me?" she said with a grin when she reached Carter's table. "My mom and I just got here. So did the Delaneys." She nodded toward the door where a tall man with piercing black eyes and black hair flecked with white stood next to a younger man in a wheelchair.

The tall man was Mr. Delaney. A volunteer Little League pitching coach, he'd taught Carter to throw the knuckleball. His son, Matt, was a former high school pitching star who now worked with the local Little League Challenger team. Carter had often wondered what had happened to put him in a wheelchair. He didn't ask, though. He thought it might be too painful for Matt to talk about.

Carter waved to the Delaneys and then asked Rachel if she wanted to sit down.

"Can't," Rachel replied. "No outsiders allowed. I just sneaked in to say hi and to give you this." She passed him a handmade book.

"What is it?" He started to leaf through it, but she stopped him.

"Don't look at it now. Just keep it with your stuff in the dugout. If you start getting all squirrelly inside, look at it then. Okay?"

"Okay." Carter tucked the book into a pocket of his gear bag.

Rachel nodded with satisfaction, then wished him

and the other players good luck and headed back to the Delaneys.

"I still say she's your girlfriend," Craig said mischievously.

Carter rolled his eyes. "Give it a rest, will you?"

CHAPTER FIVE

Liam pounded on Melanie's bedroom door. "Game day! Rise and shine!" he yelled.

He heard a muffled groan and the sound of shuffling footsteps. Then the door opened.

"Aaah!" Liam flung up his hands in mock horror. "The zombie girl awakes!"

Melanie's appearance was usually picture-perfect. But this Saturday morning, she looked like something the cat dragged in. Her hair was a tangled mess, her grungy, oversize T-shirt was half-tucked into her sleep shorts, and she was missing a slipper.

"Li-am," she complained. "Why'd you wake me up so early?"

"It's almost eleven o'clock," Liam informed her. "We're leaving for the tournament in half an hour."

She glowered at him. "Why'd you wake me up so late?" She pushed past him and dashed into the bathroom. A moment later, the shower kicked on.

Liam went downstairs to check his gear bag for the tenth time. The Sectional tournament site was only forty-five minutes away, close enough that they didn't have to stay in a hotel, but too far to return home if he forgot anything important. Satisfied that he had everything he needed, he prowled around the living room and then wandered into his parents' office.

His father was there, working on the laptop. "Hey, kiddo. You ready?"

"Yep."

Mr. McGrath swiveled around in his chair and regarded Liam closely. "And how did things go with you and Phillip these last few days?"

Liam shrugged. "Mr. Madding says we're getting there."

Mr. Madding was Ravenna's assistant coach. He'd worked with Liam and Phillip at practice Thursday and Friday. In addition to offering a few pointers, he made sure Phillip kept his pitch count low.

Liam knew that the pitch-count rules were important because they protected young pitchers' arms from common overuse injuries. Still, he wished he and Phillip had had more time to work out the kinks.

"You're not a well-oiled machine yet," the coach told them the day before, "but all the parts are in place and working. You'll be fine."

Fine. In Liam's opinion, that word meant the same thing as *average*—and average wouldn't get them very far on the road to Williamsport.

He thought about that as he followed his father into the kitchen for a quick snack. In the two days of practice, he'd done everything Phillip had asked of him— and kept his mouth shut throughout.

And I'll keep it shut, if that's what it takes to bump us from fine to great, he thought as he spread mayonnaise on a slice of wheat bread and topped it with a few slices of turkey. *Even if it kills me!*

Soon after lunch, the McGraths piled into the car and left for the tournament. Liam's bag was at his feet; Melanie had put her video equipment in the trunk. Liam was relieved that she didn't plan to pepper him with questions about Phillip during the drive. He stuck in his earbuds, adjusted the volume on his music player, and tuned out.

Forty-five minutes later, Mr. McGrath pulled into

a huge parking lot. Dozens of kids in colorful Little League uniforms from different teams were milling around, talking and laughing excitedly. In the distance, a bright green riding lawn mower droned around the outfield of one baseball diamond while sprinklers wet the infield of another to keep down the dust.

"Can you drop me off here, Dad?" Liam asked.

"Sure thing."

Mr. McGrath stopped the car under some trees. Liam grabbed his bag, jumped out, and hurried off to find the other Ravenna players. Shouted greetings pinpointed their location in the sea of people.

"Over here, McGrath!"

"Hey, Liam, 'bout time you made it!"

Liam wove his way through the crowd to his teammates. Dr. Driscoll and Mr. Madding were there, too. They told their players to stay put while they went to check in.

Dominic Blackburn, starting shortstop for that day's game, pulled Liam aside. "Don't freak out," he murmured, "but those guys from Malden keep looking at you and whispering. Oh, shoot," he added suddenly. "Here they come."

With that, Dom slipped away.

Three boys in maroon uniforms with the name

MALDEN emblazoned in white across their chests approached Liam. "Yo," the biggest of the trio said, crossing his meaty arms over his chest, "are you Liam McGrath?"

"Yeah," Liam replied warily.

The Malden players exchanged glances. "The same Liam McGrath who face-planted after striking out in the World Series?" the boy asked.

Liam's heart sank. *Not again,* he thought.

Liam's strikeout during the U.S. Championship had been devastating for three reasons. One, because it had lost his team the game. Two, because he'd swung so hard he corkscrewed around and fell face-first in the dirt. And three, because someone had captured the whole thing on tape and posted it on the Internet not long afterward.

While Little League players rarely made fun of one another, every so often, when coaches were out of earshot, one would deliver a snide comment meant to embarrass another.

There were no coaches in sight just then, so Liam steeled himself for ridicule.

But to his surprise, the boy stuck out his hand for Liam to shake. "It is you, isn't it? My name's Sam Witherspoon. I faced DiMaggio in Sectionals last year." He nodded toward his friends. "So did Tony and Ed. We're all great hitters—that's not bragging. It's a fact; you can check our stats—but none of us could get a hit off him."

Tony leaned in. "Don't tell anyone I said this," he muttered with a slight lisp, "but we were rooting for you when you batted against Phillip last August. So when you fanned . . ." He shook his head regretfully.

Liam relaxed. These boys weren't there to mock him; they were there to commiserate. "Not my greatest moment," he admitted. "But I got my swing back this spring." He cracked a smile. "I even hit a few off of ol' DiMaggio."

The three Malden players murmured appreciatively. "But now you're his teammate, right?" Sam looked to where Phillip stood talking with Dom. "Man, how can you stand it? I mean, the guy who—well, you know."

Liam took off his cap and ran a hand through his thick brown hair to buy himself time to think how best to answer. Sam and his friends were so sympathetic it was hard not to blurt out his frustrations with Phillip.

But he kept quiet. For better or worse, he and Phillip were teammates. Loyalty to the team, if nothing else, forbade him from bad-mouthing Phillip.

"I had a choice," he finally said. "I could be DiMaggio's teammate and play ball, or I could quit." He gave

Sam a lopsided grin. "I'm not a quitter and I love playing ball, so pretty easy decision, you know?"

Sam returned his smile. "You're all right, McGrath." His smile broadened. "Too bad you and your teammates are going down today!"

"You're all right, too, Witherspoon," Liam responded. "Too bad you're going to eat those words after you lose!"

They all cracked up. Then Sam, Tony, and Ed left to rejoin their teammates.

A moment later, Phillip and Dom appeared. "What did *they* want?" Phillip asked, jerking his chin at the Malden players.

"Nothing," Liam said. "Just being friendly."

Phillip and Dom exchanged disbelieving looks. Then Phillip said, "Plenty of time to be friendly—*after* we beat them."

CHAPTER
SIX

Coach Harrison bounced on the balls of his feet. "Okay, boys, round up."

Carter, Ash, and their teammates gathered in a circle by the dugout with Mr. Harrison and his assistants, Mr. Filbert and Mr. Walker.

"Hands in the middle," Mr. Harrison said. "And—"

"Forest Park, one-two-three! Forest Park, one-two-three!" the boys bellowed, flinging their hands skyward in unison on the second *three*.

It was four o'clock on Saturday afternoon—game time. The Forest Park All-Stars were facing the team from the town of Calder. Forest Park was up first.

Mr. Filbert barked out the batting order. "Detweiler, O'Donnell, Ruckel!"

Second baseman Freddie Detweiler shoved a batting helmet over his stick-straight brown hair and chose a bat.

"Go get 'em, Fredzo!" cried Raj Turner, Freddie's best friend and the game's third baseman.

Freddie flashed a big smile. His new braces, complete with plastic bands that matched the team colors of forest-green and white, glinted in the late-afternoon sun. He did indeed "get 'em," knocking out a single between first and second.

First baseman Keith O'Donnell was up next. Part Irish, part Scottish, the eleven-year-old had the freckles, thick reddish-brown hair, and pale skin common to his ancestors. He also had a stubborn streak that ran a mile deep. At one practice, he'd muffed a catch to first—and then refused to leave the field until he'd made the same catch successfully twenty times in a row.

He practiced his hitting with the same tenacity. That practice paid off now. *Crack!* The ball rocketed past Calder's shortstop. Keith reached first and Freddie landed safely at second.

Craig Ruckel, a two-time All-Star, came to the plate—and struck out swinging. Back in the dugout, he complained that the sun had blinded him.

"I should wear that black stuff under my eyes," he grumbled. "I really should."

"Coach Walker has some," Raj volunteered.

Craig grunted but didn't move from the bench. Raj caught Carter's eye and grinned. Carter shrugged. Sometimes Craig complained just for the sake of complaining.

Charlie Murray batted cleanup. Another returning All-Star, he was one of the fastest kids on the Forest Park team. He didn't need extra speed this time, though. After tapping the ball foul three times, he socked a rainmaker that soared high and dropped between center and right fields. Bases loaded, one out.

Ash was up after Charlie. Little League doesn't have an on-deck circle, but while Charlie was at the plate, Ash took practice cuts with a pretend bat. When Charlie reached first, Ash grabbed a real bat and hustled toward the batter's box.

"Play is to any base!" the Calder catcher reminded his teammates.

Carter sat forward and rubbed his suddenly sweaty palms down the front of his thighs. *Come on, Ash, get a hit!* he pleaded silently.

A single now would get them on the board first. That would be a huge boost for the team. Plus, Carter was up next. If Ash got a hit, then he would come to the plate with one out instead of two. And finally, a solid hit would give Ash a confidence boost. Every player, no matter how good, could use that.

Ash let the first pitch go by for strike one. The next pitch, though—*crack!* He connected for a knee-high line drive.

The crowd cheered—and then gasped when the pitcher made a desperate sideways lunge, snared the ball before it hit the ground, and then flipped it to Calder's first baseman. Double play!

"Great blast, Ash!" Rachel's voice rang out from the stands. "You'll get 'em next time!"

Ash stormed into the dugout, clearly disappointed, and started pulling on his catcher's gear. Carter tried to break the tension. "Hey, Ash, I—"

Ash cut him off. "Forget it. Let's go over their order again." He rattled off the names and most recent batting efforts of the first three Calder hitters. "Larry Miller: bats righty, hit three singles and a double, struck out twice, popped out, and grounded out twice in Calder's bid to be District champs. Jarvis Greenaway: bats righty, one homer, two singles, four strikeouts, very fast on the base paths. Ricky Muldoon: bats righty, two

44

singles, a triple, grounded out four times. He could be dangerous."

"Not to us."

Ash looked up then. Carter handed him his catcher's helmet and smiled encouragingly. After a second, Ash stood up. "Yeah, not to us."

"You boys ready?" Coach Harrison called out.

"Absolutely!" Carter said. He grabbed his glove and raced out to the mound.

And he was. Maybe it was the perfect baseball weather. Maybe it was the fact that the stands were packed with familiar faces—his parents, Rachel, the Delaneys, and lots of kids from his hometown Little League. Maybe it was simply that he and Ash had been playing together as pitcher and catcher for months. Whatever the reason, he took to the mound with confidence coursing through his veins.

Larry Miller stepped into the box. Carter sized him up and then nodded at Ash's signal for a fastball high and tight. He reared back and threw. Larry swung and missed.

"Strike one!"

Two more strikes sent Larry back to the dugout. It took just three more pitches to strike out Jarvis Greenaway, too.

Ricky Muldoon came up with a little swagger in his step. He returned Carter's stare-down with a fierce look of his own. Not that it did him any good. *Swish! Swish! Swish!* He took three monstrous cuts and hit nothing but air.

I just retired the side with nine straight pitches, Carter thought with amazement.

A few of his teammates smiled at him as they trotted into the dugout. But to his puzzlement, no one congratulated him. Not that he needed praise, but he'd assumed Ash or Coach Harrison at least would comment on the three-up, three-down inning.

What the heck? he thought as he tried and failed to catch Ash's eye.

Then it hit him. He sank down on the end of the bench, his heart hammering in his chest.

I'm one inning into a no-hitter!

Baseball, like any sport, has many superstitious beliefs. The superstition surrounding a no-hitter is among the most sacred. Players and fans of all ages believe that merely mentioning a no-hitter could jinx the pitcher. Many refuse to talk to the pitcher at all for fear of accidentally putting a whammy on his streak.

"Jones!"

Carter snapped back to the present. He gulped when he saw Mr. Filbert beckoning to him.

He's going to say something to me about the...the... Carter refused to even think the word.

To his profound relief, the coach simply held out a helmet and said, "You're up first."

CHAPTER
SEVEN

An hour before game time, Ravenna, Malden, and the two other teams in the Sectional tournament, Seaport and Yorkshire, took to the field for the opening ceremonies. The players stood behind each team's District Championship banner and, caps held over their hearts, listened respectfully as an elderly man sang the national anthem. The same man then invited them to say the Little League pledge in unison.

After Liam repeated his promise to play fairly and try his best, he glanced around at his teammates. Most wore similar expressions of eagerness and excitement. He caught Phillip's eye and, after a brief hesitation, offered him a smile. Phillip nodded once.

When the pledge finished, the man in charge made a short speech about the tournament. "Game One is Malden versus Ravenna on Field One. Seaport and Yorkshire will be on the other diamond. Tomorrow, the two winners will face each other, as will the teams that lose today. This is a double-elimination format. When a team loses twice, it is out."

He paused a moment to let that information sink in. Then he reminded everyone to respect the umpires and the players at all times. Finally, he instructed the teams to head to their fields for the pregame warm-ups.

Ravenna, the home team, had fielding practice first. Liam had played all six innings in the final District game, so he wasn't in the starting lineup. Phillip, Cole Dudley, and Carmen Baker were subs, too. They joined their teammates in the outfield, though, because they would all see playing time sooner or later. For his part, Liam hoped it would be sooner.

After fifteen minutes, the head umpire, a heavy-set man with a shock of white hair and a no-nonsense demeanor, ordered Ravenna off and Malden on. A short time later, the two teams switched places again and the game began.

Elton Sears, a strong pitcher with a sizzling fastball, started Ravenna off well by delivering three pitches that were right on the money. The Malden player swung at all three. He missed the first, fouled the second, and fanned at the third for out number one.

The next batter was Tony, one of the boys Liam had met earlier. Sam had said that Tony was a good hitter. Part of Liam's job as a catcher was to recognize batting threats. There was no guarantee he'd ever be playing catcher when Tony was at bat, but still...

Better pay attention, he thought, leaning forward, elbows on knees, to watch Tony.

He didn't have much opportunity to study him, however. Tony let Elton's first two pitches go by. Both were balls. With the count two-and-oh, Liam didn't expect Tony to swing at the third. But Elton must have thrown something Tony liked, for when the pitch came, the Malden player took a big cut at it.

Crack!

The ball jumped off the bat and soared to right-center field. Liam and the other players leaped to their feet, shouting encouragement to the outfielders.

Rodney streaked across from the right. Matt Finch, playing center field this game, raced over, too. It should have been Matt's catch; he was closer and the ball was falling on his glove side. But suddenly, he tripped and went sprawling across the grass.

Groans of sympathy mixed with disappointment rose from Ravenna's fans. No doubt they thought the hit would go for at least a single now.

But they hadn't counted on Rodney. When Matt fell, Rodney put on a burst of speed. At the last second, he dove, arm outstretched, and caught the ball bare-handed!

"Yes!" Liam whooped. He could hear Sean shouting from the stands. Cole and Carmen jumped up and slapped high five. Coach Driscoll folded his arms over his chest, his face shining with pride.

Phillip, meanwhile, clapped and smiled with satisfaction. His eyes followed Rodney as the outfielder trotted back to his spot. Then he looked at Liam appraisingly. "Now *that's* an All-Star," he said. He held Liam's gaze for a moment longer before turning away.

Liam blinked. He completely agreed with Phillip about Rodney. After that fantastic catch, who wouldn't? But for some reason, the comment bothered him.

Because it seemed as if he was saying you aren't an All-Star, a little voice inside him whispered.

Liam frowned at the thought. It was crazy, after all. He was just as much an All-Star as Rodney.

Except you're only on this bench because someone else dropped out, the little voice mocked. *You're only getting to play catcher because Owen can't. No wonder DiMaggio keeps correcting how you play!*

Liam looked sideways at Phillip.

"What?" Phillip said when he caught the look.

"Nothing. Just . . . nothing."

Rodney's circus catch set the tone for the next innings. In the field, the Ravenna players chased down balls, fired pinpoint throws, and reacted to situations with clockwork efficiency. At bat, they lit up the starting pitcher and the one who replaced him, too. When Liam took over for Nate Solis in left field at the top of the fourth, the score was Ravenna 6, Malden 1.

The other subs got in the game, too. Phillip was in the hot corner, third base. Cole replaced Luis Cervantes at catcher, with Carmen relieving Elton on the mound.

Sometimes such lineup changes can break a team's rhythm. When Carmen gave up a home run to Sam, Liam tensed. Was this the beginning of a Malden rally?

It wasn't. The next three hitters made outs. Ravenna 6, Malden 2.

Liam led off in the bottom of the fourth. He took a deep breath, stepped into the box—and creamed the first pitch for a stand-up double!

After that, Malden fell apart. Its fielders made

unforced errors. Its batters swung at pitches that were far outside the strike zone. Ravenna, meanwhile, racked up three more runs. The game ended after five and a half innings with a final score of Ravenna 9, Malden 2.

In the postgame hand-slap, Liam shook Sam's hand. "Good game, man. And good luck tomorrow."

"Thanks," Sam replied. "Here's hoping we meet again." He gave Liam a rueful smile.

Liam nodded his understanding. They'd meet again only if Malden won the next day's match. Lose, and Malden was out of the tournament. Liam liked Sam. He hoped his team performed better tomorrow than it had that afternoon. But if not, well...only one team could come out on top.

CHAPTER
EIGHT

Carter had hoped to start the second inning with a hit. He grounded out.

"Good try, Carter," Coach Harrison said. "Raj, you're up."

Raj was a slender boy with a mop of shiny black hair. A year younger and a foot shorter than Carter, he bore an unfortunate resemblance to a bobblehead whenever he wore a batting helmet.

"I'm not a power hitter," he once confided in Carter with a forlorn look at his thin arms and bony wrists. "So I try to follow Wee Willie Keeler's advice."

"'Hit 'em where they ain't'?" Carter guessed, remembering the Hall of Famer's best-known quote.

"Exactly."

Raj hit a tumbling grounder that bounced between shortstop and third. The third baseman nabbed the ball and fired it to first. It should have been a straightforward putout—but the throw was wild! Raj touched first and continued on to second.

Allen Avery drew a walk. With runners on first and second and one out, Charlie Santiago socked the ball deep into left field. Raj and Allen churned up the base paths. When the dust settled, Raj had crossed home, Allen was standing on third, Charlie was safe at second, and Forest Park had its first run on the board.

That's all they got that inning. Allen and Charlie were left stranded on base when Freddie and Keith popped out one after the other. Still, the mood in the dugout was upbeat when the runners returned.

"Nice blast, Charlie S.," Charlie Murray praised.

The center fielder grinned. "Thanks, Charlie M. And nice running, Raj. You too, Allen." He grabbed his glove and added, "Now if Carter can just keep—ooof!"

Charlie S.'s breath came out in a whoosh thanks to a jab in the ribs from Ash. "What's the big idea?" he demanded, glaring at Ash.

Ash glared back. After a second, Charlie's eyes widened. He clapped a hand over his mouth, glanced at

Carter, and then ran from the dugout without saying another word.

Carter left the dugout in a hurry, before anyone else accidentally mentioned the no-hitter. That's when the jitters struck.

Okay, calm down, he said to himself. He remembered Liam's saying how deep breaths helped him focus. So he inhaled and exhaled, slowly and evenly. With each breath, his anxiety eased a little. When the first Calder batter stepped into the box, he was ready.

More than ready—he was on fire. Three sizzling fastballs. Three swings a fraction too late. One out.

The second batter grounded out after five pitches. The third reached for a changeup and missed. He nicked the second pitch, but the ball flew foul. So did the next three. Finally, he straightened one out, but it was just a weak pop fly toward short. Allen caught the ball easily.

Another hitless inning. Back in the dugout, Carter felt as if he were sitting inside a protective bubble. No one, not even the coaches, came near him.

The top of the third inning began with Craig reaching first on a walk and ended with another run on Forest Park's side after Raj hit an RBI double. Back on the mound, Carter retired the remaining three batters of Calder's lineup in order.

Three innings played, nine batters faced, no hits made, and no one reached base. Carter wasn't just pitching a no-hitter; he was halfway to a perfect game!

As they jogged off the field, Carter's teammates darted quick glances at him but said nothing. Carter sat on the bench, closed his eyes, and breathed slowly. But this time, the calming technique didn't help. The dugout was too charged with repressed excitement.

Then, just as tension started to freeze the blood in his veins, he heard Rachel bellow, "Go, Forest Park, go!"

Carter suddenly remembered the book she'd given him. He pulled it out and opened it. On the first page, there was a cartoon illustration of a pitcher in the midst of his windup. The pitcher looked a lot like him—left-handed and green-eyed, with shaggy brown hair peeking out from under a forest-green baseball cap.

Why does a pitcher raise one leg when he throws? the caption read.

He flipped to the next page.

Because if he raised two, he'd fall down!

The joke was awful, but the illustration of the dazed pitcher sprawled on the mound was hilarious. At the bottom of the page, she'd added another thought: *You're going to fall sometimes, you know. Just get back up again!*

The corner of his mouth twitched in a half smile.

Throughout the regular Little League season, Rachel had kept him loose by cracking stupid jokes whenever they were on the bench. She wasn't allowed in the dugout now, but her book proved a good substitute. Carter slowly relaxed.

Thanks, Rach, he thought as he put the book away.

Forest Park added two more runs its turn at bat. In the bottom of the fourth, Carter faced the triple threats of Larry, Jarvis, and Ricky again. He struck Larry out but gave up a walk to Jarvis—and then one to Ricky as well.

Ash called time and hurried to the mound. He gave Carter an appraising look and then said, "I've been thinking about that fist-bump thing you and Liam do."

Carter blinked in surprise. "Yeah, so?"

"So, you do it for luck, right? Thing is, you don't need luck." The catcher gripped Carter's shoulder. "You don't need luck because you have talent. Loads and loads of talent. Talent is what wins games, not luck. So shake off the walks and bring on the heat, okay?"

Carter grinned. "Okay."

Two batters later, the no-hitter was still alive.

Alive—but as of the top of the fifth inning, in someone else's hands.

"You're at forty-nine pitches," Coach Harrison

informed Carter. "Any more, and it's unlikely you can pitch again this tournament. So Peter's going to take it from here."

Carter's face fell. "Oh. Okay."

Disappointed, he barely noticed when Forest Park failed to get on base, though he snapped back to attention when Peter Molina took the mound. He held his breath with every pitch, letting it out only after Larry Miller, the top of Calder's batting order, made the third out to end the fifth hitless inning.

Forest Park didn't add more runs its final turn at bat. With the score at 4–0, Calder had one last chance to get on the board.

The first batter was Jarvis Greenaway. He didn't deliver. Next up was Ricky Muldoon. He took two called strikes and then—*pow!* He belted the third into the clear blue sky. The ball soared as far as it did high, dropping beyond the outfield fence when it finally came back to earth.

Forest Park 4, Calder 1.

CHAPTER
NINE

Oh, man, Carter, that rots."

Liam had been in the shower when he'd heard the blooping tones from his laptop, the signal that he had an incoming video-chat call. He'd thrown on a T-shirt and shorts, but his hair was still wet. He slicked it back now, sending a rain of droplets down his back.

"I still can't get used to you with Bieber hair," Carter commented. When Liam lived in Pennsylvania, he'd worn his hair in a closely cropped crew cut. Since moving to California, he'd let it grow out, so now it was as long as teen music superstar Justin Bieber's famous mop.

"It's not Bieber hair," Liam protested. "It's just hair.

And don't change the subject. You always do that when you don't want to talk about something."

"Duh, doofus, that's why it's called 'changing the subject,'" Carter said, rolling his eyes.

"Yeah, well, we're not going to do that this time. I know you're bummed out. But at least you won the game, right?"

Carter nodded. "And I'm not that bummed out—okay, fine, I am," he amended when Liam snorted. "But you should have seen Peter. He pretty much lost it after the game. Must have apologized to me a hundred times."

"What did you—"

Carter interrupted him. "Hang on a second." He disappeared from Liam's screen. Liam heard a door open and the sound of voices. Then Carter returned. "Sorry about that. Ash forgot his key card."

Liam was momentarily confused. Then he remembered Carter was sharing a hotel room with Ash during the tournament.

"Oh, hey, Liam," Ash said, peering over Carter's shoulder at the screen. He jerked his head toward Carter. "He tell you about the near no-hitter?"

"Yeah," Liam replied. "And about how wrecked Peter was for giving up that homer. So what did you do when he apologized?" He directed the question to Carter, but Ash answered.

"He told Peter it was okay, that these things happen, and that he shouldn't feel bad about it." Ash pulled a face. "You ask me, he was too easy on him."

I wasn't asking you, Liam was tempted to say. Instead, he flicked a significant look at Carter. Carter started toying with a loose thread on his shirt.

"So tell me, Ash, what would *you* have done?" Liam knew he sounded sarcastic, but he didn't care. Ash was getting on his nerves, first for barging in on their chat and now for making Carter feel bad for treating Peter with grace. As if Carter knew how to behave any differently!

"Listen," Ash said, pitching his voice in a reasonable tone that made Liam only more annoyed, "all I'm saying is that the challenges and the pressure are only going to be greater the further we go on the road to Williamsport. The better prepared Peter is for it, the better off our team will be."

With that, he moved out of camera range. A moment later, Liam heard the hotel room door close.

Neither Carter nor Liam said anything for a few seconds. Then Carter sighed. "He has a point."

"Yeah. And it's right on the top of his head."

That got a smile from his cousin. Liam was about to remind him that it was Coach Harrison's job to talk to Peter, not Ash's or Carter's, but there was a loud knock at the hotel door.

Liam grimaced. "What, did he forget his key card again?"

Carter vanished once more. This time when he returned, it was a girl who joined him on-screen.

"Hey, I remember you," she said, a wide smile lighting up her face. "You're Liam."

"And you're Rachel, right?" Liam had never been in class with Rachel when he lived in Pennsylvania, but he still recognized her. Plus, Carter had talked about her enough that he was sure that's who the girl was. He remembered what Carter had said about his former Hawks teammate, too. "You're the one with all the bad jokes."

"Not all of them," Rachel rejoined mischievously. "Carter says you have plenty yourself. Listen, Carter, I'm sorry for the intrusion, but I got some great news and I couldn't wait until morning to tell you." Eyes shining with excitement, she announced, "I'm going to the Little League World Series!"

Liam stared at her in confusion. So did Carter.

"Don't take this the wrong way," Carter said, "but... *huh?*"

Rachel burst out laughing. "With our Challenger team, as a buddy!"

In 1989, Little League created a new program known as the Challenger Division. Teams were made up of physically and developmentally disabled players. Most of the players had "buddies"—Little Leaguers from different divisions—who helped them play games.

"Matt's team is one of the two playing in the Challenger Game at Williamsport during the World Series," Rachel explained. "I couldn't go at first because we were going on vacation that week. But my parents changed our plans, so now I can!"

"That's great," Carter said enthusiastically.

"And you know what else is great about it? I'll be there when Forest Park wins the World Series this year!"

"Hey now!" Liam interjected. "Who says his team will make the title game? Ravenna could wipe out Forest Park in the U.S. Championship, remember!"

He meant it as a joke. But all at once, what he said struck home.

Before the postseason began, he and Carter had speculated about the possibility that their teams might meet in Williamsport. They'd agreed that the odds were stacked against it. After all, the same teams had never faced each other in the U.S. Championship two years in a row.

But now that both had won their first games in Sectionals, the odds were starting to look a little more favorable.

Rachel cleared her throat. "Well, one thing's for sure. No matter what happens, you two will always be each other's biggest fan. Right?"

"Absolutely," Carter said.

"One hundred percent right," Liam agreed without hesitation.

The three chatted for a bit longer. When Carter gave a huge yawn, Liam remembered that while it was only seven o'clock in California, it was already ten in Pennsylvania.

"Let's wrap it up," he said. He held up his fist. Carter did the same. They tapped their screens three times. Then Carter and Rachel's image winked out.

Alone in his room, Liam twisted around on his bed and stared at a photograph hanging above his head-board. Carter had given him the picture for Christmas, just before he moved to California. It was an aerial view of his hometown in Pennsylvania. He could see Carter's house and, two roofs down, the house where he used to live—and where Ash now lived.

Liam made a face. *Ash. Ashley. How can Carter stand to be on a team with him? Well, one thing's for sure. If Forest Park does get to the World Series, I'll be cheering for Carter. But Ash?* He shook his head. *Maybe not so much.*

CHAPTER
TEN

On Sunday, Forest Park faced Groveland for its second Sectional game. Carter played third base for three innings and got up to bat twice. When the score jumped to 8–0 in Forest Park's favor, Coach Harrison took him out. Carter didn't mind. If they won that day, they'd play again on Tuesday. He understood the coach wanted him well rested for that game because he'd be taking the mound again.

Three innings later, his team did indeed win. Final score: Forest Park 10, Groveland 2.

Rachel bounded up to Carter after the game, full of congratulations. "I wish I could stay for the rest of the tourney," she said. "But Mom's working tomorrow, so we're heading back now."

"Thanks for coming, Rach," Carter said. "And thanks for the book, too."

Rachel grinned. When her mother called for her, she gave Carter a high five and then vanished into the crowd.

A few minutes later Mr. Delaney appeared, pushing Matt in his wheelchair. They congratulated Carter and then Matt stage-whispered conspiratorially, "I see you've kept your secret weapon under wraps so far. Good move."

Carter laughed. He knew Matt was referring to the knuckleball. He hadn't used it in the game against Calder because he'd been successful with his fastball and changeup. "Coach Harrison thought it made sense to keep that one up my sleeve, just in case we faced Calder again."

"He's a smart one, that man." The Delaneys shook his hand, wished him good luck in his next game, and then departed.

Back in his hotel room, Carter did a quick calculation and realized Liam was likely home from his game by now. He tried to video-chat with him. But the Internet connection wasn't working, so, instead, he found out via text message that Liam's team had won its second game as well.

If we win on Tuesday, Liam's text read, *we're heading to the SoCal S SDs!*

"SoCal S SDs" stood for the Southern California South Sub-Divisional Tournament. Because the state was so large, California had two Little League divisions, one in the north and one in the south. Northern California was further divided into NoCal North and NoCal South; likewise, Southern California was split into SoCal North and SoCal South.

Ravenna was in SoCal South. If the team beat the competition in its section, it would advance to the Sub-Division tournament and play other SoCal South section winners. If Ravenna won there, it would play a single game against the winner from SoCal North. And if it emerged victorious over SoCal North, it would represent the Southern California Division at the Western Regional Tournament.

Carter was happy for Liam, and even happier that Forest Park's Sunday win had earned the team a bye on Monday. Monday morning, he and his father were the first ones in the hotel pool.

"I challenge you to a race," Carter said. He tightened his swim goggles and then called out, "On your mark, get set—GO!"

Father and son shoved off from the side of the pool, arms chopping through the chlorinated water and legs kicking up a splash behind. Mr. Jones touched the edge first, whirled around, and started to stroke his way back to the other end. Carter was close to catching him when, suddenly, the strap on his goggles snapped. He finished the race without them and came up laughing.

"I demand a rematch! Where are my goggles?"

Mr. Jones fished them out of the water. "Here you go." But when Carter reached for them, his father playfully yanked them out of reach. "Oops! Too slow!"

Carter was still trying to grab his goggles when he spied Ash on their balcony. He jumped high out of the water and waved for him to join them. Ash glanced down, then turned away and disappeared into their room. Carter was sure he had seen him. But when he didn't come down to the pool, he decided he must have been wrong.

Monday afternoon, the Forest Park team gathered in the stands to watch Calder play Groveland. Ash had his baseball binder with him. Throughout the game, he added information on the pages marked *Calder* and *Groveland.*

"Do you toss the stuff about the losing teams?" Carter asked curiously.

"I never toss anything," Ash replied. "Kids who play for losing teams one year might be on winning teams in the next." He flipped to a different page and tapped a photo of a boy. "Case in point."

Carter glanced at the photo—and blinked in surprise. "Hey, that's me from last year's World Series!"

Ash nodded. "I told you when we first met that I already knew a lot about you, remember? Well, I wasn't lying. I got the picture off the Internet. The info I got by watching games and reading articles."

"No way! Let me see."

Carter took the binder and read about himself with fascination. There was little about last year's regular season or District tournament, but Ash had compiled plenty of facts and figures about his performances in Sectionals, States, Regionals, and of course, the World Series.

He'd added personal observations, too. One note in particular, about his habit of throwing the ball into his glove over and over, jumped out at Carter.

Shows he's nervous? Ash had written. *If so, better to let him work it out this way.*

Carter made a face. He hadn't realized his habit revealed so much about his state of mind. If Ash had picked up on it, others probably had, too, or could if they hadn't already. He resolved then and there to quit doing it.

He turned to the next page, expecting to see a new player's profile. Instead, he found himself staring at a long list of players he'd struck out. The list started with last year's postseason and continued through his near no-hitter over Calder. Seen as a whole, the stats overwhelmed him.

"*Now* do you get why I wanted to be your catcher?" Ash asked quietly. "You're not a good Little League pitcher, Carter. You're an ace."

Dumbfounded, Carter just shook his head, closed the book, and handed it back to Ash without a word. He watched the rest of the game in a fog. Calder won big, 11–3.

Carter finally snapped back to attention during the announcements about the Sectional title game scheduled for the next morning. The head of the tournament stood at home plate, microphone in hand, and addressed the players and people gathered in the stands.

"Calder now has a record of two wins and one loss. Forest Park's record stands at two wins and no losses," he stated. "The final matchup between these two worthy teams will begin tomorrow on this field at eleven sharp."

He paused then, for a woman was hurrying out to convey a whispered message. The man glanced up at the sky and then addressed the crowd again. "Folks, it seems the morning's weather forecast is calling for passing thunderstorms. So that eleven o'clock start time might not happen. Coaches, be sure to check the tournament hotline for any postponements. We'll get the information there first thing tomorrow."

"Man, I hope those weather guys are wrong," Raj said to Carter as they clattered down the bleachers and started back to the hotel. "I'm ready to take on Calder right now! Aren't you?"

Carter flashed back to Ash's binder. In his mind's eye, he saw the line of Ks, the shorthand symbol for strikeouts, marching next to all the players he'd fanned. Some of those players were on Calder.

"Yeah," he replied to Raj. "I'm ready."

CHAPTER
ELEVEN

Eight o'clock Tuesday morning, Liam rose from his bed and stared out his window. A layer of light gray clouds scudded across the sky, thick enough to block the sun but not threaten rain. In other words, good baseball weather, for no sun in the sky meant no sun in the eyes.

The sun stayed hidden throughout breakfast and the forty-five-minute car ride to the tournament. Liam was walking to the ball field for Ravenna's pregame warm-ups when Sean caught up to him.

"I just got a call from Carter," Sean informed Liam. "His game has been postponed to the late afternoon because of a thunderstorm. So he wants me to text him a play-by-play of your game. Can I use your phone? Mine's almost out of battery."

Liam had planned on giving his phone to his mother to hold since he couldn't have it with him in the dugout. But he was more than happy to give it to Sean. "Make sure you get a good seat in the bleachers. If you can, film the best plays and send him those, too." He showed him how to reach the video feature on his phone.

"How will I know what the best plays are?" Sean asked.

Liam puffed out his chest with exaggerated bravado. "Those will be the ones I'm part of. So keep it rolling if I'm at or behind the plate."

Melanie, walking right behind them, must have overheard their conversation, because she cut in. "I'll be filming stuff, too," she reminded her brother. "If Sean misses something, I'll have it."

Liam turned to Sean and said with mock amazement, "Well, what do you know. She's good for something after all."

"Watch it, mister," Melanie growled. She patted her video camera. "Remember, I've already got lots of footage of some of your 'best plays.'"

Liam eyed her warily. "Such as?"

She gave him a crafty smile. "That's for me to know and you to find out—*if* I decide to let you find out."

Liam wasn't sure he liked the sound of that. But he didn't have time to question her more because he was due on the field. Their practice time was particularly important this game because he was catching for Phillip.

The two had worked together over the past few days. Mr. Madding had been on hand at all times and had upgraded his evaluation of their progress from "fine" to "very good."

In Liam's opinion, though, things were still off. Phillip had finally run out of suggestions. Liam thought he'd be happy when that happened. But now the only communication they had were pitch signals, nods, and the occasional "hey."

"It's like catching for a pitching machine," he told his mother in exasperation after Monday's brief practice, "except the machine at least goes *thup* when it releases the ball."

Mrs. McGrath smiled. "And what sounds do you make?" she teased.

"Ha, ha," he replied sarcastically.

"What I mean is, are *you* talking to *him*?"

Liam huffed out a huge sigh. "What am I supposed to say?"

She patted him on the hand and stood up to start fixing dinner. "I'm sure when the time is right, you'll find the words."

Despite his mother's confidence, silence still reigned between Liam and Phillip going into Tuesday's game. After warm-ups, Liam took his place behind the plate and Phillip hustled to the mound without exchanging much more than a "good luck."

The game that morning was against Malden again. Since its loss to Ravenna, Malden had crushed Seaport and Yorkshire, racking up scores in the double digits in both games while giving up fewer than six total runs. Sam, Tony, and Ed proved they hadn't been bragging about their hitting abilities. Together, they were responsible for more than half of Malden's runs.

Liam had no doubt they were happy with their performances—and that they'd be happier still to sweeten their tallies with strong showings against Phillip.

But not as happy as I'll be if we send you back to the dugout without a single hit among you! he thought.

Last game, Tony batted second. This time, he was first in Malden's batting order. A classic leadoff batter, he was speedy enough to outrun the throw to first if he got even a weak hit. That's just what he got, nicking a low fastball that bounced and then rolled toward short.

Dom rushed in, glove low and ready. Somehow, though, the ball dribbled between his feet! By the time he'd spun around and nabbed it out of the grass, Tony had sprinted safely to first. He stayed there for less than a minute before his teammate sacrifice-bunted him to second.

With one out, runner on second, the third Malden batter came to the plate. Liam remembered him clearly from their previous meeting—not because he'd done anything outstanding, but because he was constantly chewing bubble gum. Liam liked gum as much as the next kid, but listening to the hitter work the pink wad over and around in his mouth made him a little queasy. Luckily, he didn't have to listen for long. The boy grounded out on the first pitch.

Sam came up next. He'd been friendly to Liam when they first met and the few times they'd seen each other since. Now, though, he didn't even glance at Liam. Liam understood—it was game time, after all.

Sam settled into his stance. Liam flashed the signal for a changeup. Phillip rubbed his face on his shoulder and then reared back and threw. Many times, the off-speed pitch fooled the batter into swinging too soon.

Not Sam. He connected and sent the ball sailing toward left field. It would have been a solid single if it hadn't flown foul. He fouled the second one as well, and then watched as Phillip's next three pitches went wide of the strike zone.

Liam's heart started racing. It was a full count, three balls, two strikes. Unless the next pitch was an obvious ball, Sam was likely to swing.

Phillip twirled the ball behind his back, his stare dark and intense. He took the signal, wound up, and threw.

Crack!

Sam's bat found the ball. The white sphere soared straight up into the air above home plate. Liam leaped up and ripped off his mask in one smooth motion.

"I've got it!" he cried.

The ball was almost invisible against the cloudy sky. He kept his eyes locked on it. Then, suddenly, the clouds parted. A ray of bright sunlight shone through like a laser beam and hit Liam right in the face! Momentarily blinded by the brilliance, he blinked rapidly, trying to clear away the afterimage and follow the ball's trajectory at the same time.

But it was no use. A split second too late, he realized the ball was falling behind him. He whirled and lunged, glove outstretched.

Plop!

The ball fell in the dirt just behind home plate. Instead of being out on a caught pop-up, Sam was still alive. He made the most of his unexpected chance, belting Phillip's next pitch. Tony scored and Sam was safe at second. He was stranded on base when the fifth Malden batter struck out, but the damage was done. Malden was on the board first.

In the dugout, Liam was busy taking off his gear when he felt the hairs on the back of his neck prickle. He glanced up and saw Phillip staring at him through narrowed eyes.

"What?" he asked.

"Your buddy Sam sure got lucky, huh?" Phillip said, and then walked away.

CHAPTER TWELVE

Carter's cell phone chimed. Even with the volume at its highest setting, he almost didn't hear it. That's because his hotel room was crammed with noisy boys.

Allen had shown up soon after the rain delay was announced. "I'm bored," he said when Carter answered the door. "The pool's closed because of the storm and another bunch of Little Leaguers are using the Ping-Pong table."

"So hang out here," Carter said, stepping aside so Allen could enter.

Charlie Murray and Charlie Santiago arrived a few minutes later, having received a text from Allen.

Charlie M. flopped down on Ash's bed. "Hey, Carter, how's Liam doing?"

Carter waved his phone in the air. "I'm going to be getting a play-by-play of the game in just a little while," he said. "I'll keep you posted."

"Awesome. All right if I tell the other guys about it?"

Before Carter could object, Charlie M. had texted the rest of the team. Now the Forest Park players were draped over every available surface of Carter and Ash's room—floor, beds, the chair someone had dragged in from the Joneses' adjoining room. The Joneses had provided lunch—deli sandwiches, chips, cookies, and drinks—and the air was ripe with the smell of pickles and potato chips. Some of the boys were watching a ball game on television while others played head-to-head video games on their portable devices. Ash sat with his back against the balcony door, his binder propped up on his knees. Carter was at the desk, phone in hand.

"Hey, guys," he said loudly when it chimed. "I got the first message."

"Read it out loud, man," Charlie M. said, muting the TV, "and pass me those cookies."

Carter handed over a sleeve of Oreos and then relayed the message: *T1: L misses pop-up at plate. Batter RBIs. Malden 1.*

Ash looked up. "Liam flubbed a catch?" When Carter confirmed the miss, Ash nodded and then made a mark in his notebook.

"Aw, no big deal," Raj said, waving dismissively. "The game just started."

That was true, but Carter knew that Liam would hate himself for making an error like that, especially in the top of the first inning—or *T1*, as Sean called it. He could picture Liam's face perfectly: stony and tight with disappointment.

Shake it off, he silently urged.

The updates from Sean came fast and furious after the first one.

B1: 4 at bats, no score. M 1, R 0.

T2: Walk. Steal—wait, no! Liam gets him!

Several players whooped at Liam's pickoff at second. "Made up for his error pretty quick," Charlie M. said.

Carter was a little puzzled over the message that followed. ":*D, 1, 1, DP*? What does that mean?"

Freddie and Luke Armstrong helped him interpret. "That's an excited face," Freddie said, pointing to the colon and capital D. "Must be for the pickoff."

"And those number ones are singles," Luke put in, "and since the inning ends after that *DP*, I bet that's double play."

"Makes sense," Carter agreed.

He got the hang of Sean's shorthand after that. When the next text came, he deciphered it quickly. "Liam led off with a double," he reported, eliciting more whoops from Liam's former teammates. "Then someone singled. The next batter popped out, and the guy after him grounded out."

"But the runners are still on base?" Allen asked.

Carter nodded just as his phone chimed again. "Yeah, and now the bases are loaded because someone singled!"

"Blast it out of the park!" Charlie S. cried.

The room fell silent as they waited to learn what happened next.

"What's taking so long?" Craig asked impatiently.

Carter's phone finally alerted him that he had a message. He read the text and the one that followed immediately after. "RBI single, Liam scores! But then the person after him struck out."

The players let out groans of disappointment. "That guy must be bumming," Peter Molina said quietly. "Who was it?"

"Not sure." Carter's thumbs roved over the phone's tiny keyboard. "Okay, I just asked Sean to send me the batting order."

Ash pushed off from the floor and moved to a spot behind Carter. "Good idea," he said. "Now we can track who their best hitters are."

He flipped to a blank page at the end of his binder and wrote *Ravenna* in block letters across the top. Then he jotted a column of numbers from one to nine, with four extra spaces for the subs.

Carter's phone chimed. "Here we go." He read off Ravenna's batting order: *Dom, Phillip, Matt, Rodney, Liam, Mason, Cole, Elton, Nate.*

"Too bad we can't see what they look like," catcher Ron Davis said.

Carter grinned. "Actually, we can." He opened his laptop, typed in his password, and then clicked the photo icon. A second later, the Ravenna District Champs team picture popped up. Listed under the photo were the players' names. He turned the laptop so everyone could see. "Ta-da!"

"You're like a spy," Raj said, gesturing to the laptop and cell phone. "The way you put that all together so fast, it was like something out of a James Bond movie."

Carter struck a debonair pose, chin in hand and a single eyebrow lifted. "The name's Jones. Carter Jones," he said in his best English accent.

"Dum duh-duh-duh-duh dum-dum, dum duh-duh-

duh-duh dum-dum." Several of the boys intoned the opening notes to the classic Bond theme song.

Ash, meanwhile, was rapidly adding the last names of the Ravenna players to his list. "So if Liam doubled," he said, tapping the paper, "that means Mason Sykes singled, Cole Dudley popped out, and Elton Sears grounded out. Then Nate Solis and Dom Blackburn singled and"—he looked up at Carter with a glint in his eye—"Phillip struck out."

Carter had been about to text Sean that he was disappointed for Ravenna. But the news that Phillip had struck out made him pause.

So the great DiMaggio ended their chances, huh?

The moment the thought crossed his mind, he felt guilty. This was Liam's team, and it had just missed a golden opportunity to add a run to its side—maybe more than one, given that the bases were loaded and Matt Finch, one of Ravenna's heavy hitters, was next in the order. He should be feeling bad for Liam, not happy that Phillip made an out.

Better luck next inning, he texted to Sean.

CHAPTER
THIRTEEN

I should say something to him.

That was the thought running through Liam's mind as he caught Phillip's warm-up throws at the top of the third inning. If it had been any pitcher but Phillip, he would have told him to put the strikeout behind him, remember that they had a run on the board, and focus on preventing Malden from adding to its score.

But because the pitcher was Phillip, he hesitated. They had barely spoken the whole tournament. What would he even say to him?

Then out of nowhere, his mother's voice came back to him. *"When the time is right, you'll find the words."*

At that same moment, the umpires announced

there would be a brief delay while first base was fixed more securely to the ground.

Liam's heart skipped a beat. What if now was the right time and he missed his chance? He couldn't risk it. He ran out to the pitcher's mound to talk to Phillip.

Phillip frowned when he saw him. "What're you doing out here?"

"I just wanted to tell you to shake off that strikeout," Liam said, ignoring the hint of animosity in Phillip's tone. "Because these Malden guys can hit and they are gunning for you. So—"

Phillip interrupted him with a derisive snort. "Geez, McGrath, you think it's big news that these batters want to hit off me? Well, it's not. Hitters have been looking to tee off me all season. Getting a blast off the World Series–winning pitcher is like winning the lottery, right?" He leaned in. "That's what you've been talking about with your Malden buddies, isn't it? About how great it was to make me eat my pitches during the regular season."

Liam stared at Phillip for a long moment. Then he shook his head. "You know what? You're right. That's exactly what I was trying to do whenever we faced each other. Know something else? It cost me my spot on the All-Star roster. You and I both know I'm only here because some other guy decided not to play. And I'm

92

your catcher today only because Owen got sidelined." He let out a long sigh. "The thing is, I'm actually a good catcher. I'd have to be to have been in the World Series, wouldn't I?"

With that, Liam started back to the plate. Then he turned around. "You think it's hard facing batters who want to hit off you? Try pretending you don't hear people whispering that you're the guy whose strikeout lost his team the World Series. Or moving across the country to the town where the pitcher who struck you out lives. Oh, and then try changing everything about the way you play your position in the hope that it will make things work with that very same pitcher. Yeah, that's fun."

The words spilled out of his mouth before he could stop them. He instantly wished them back. He'd gone out to the mound to reassure Phillip. Instead, he'd gone on a rant about how hard his own life was. Face flaming with embarrassment, he hurried back to the plate.

Malden was at the top of its batting order. Tony, up first, struck out swinging. The next two grounded out. In all, Phillip had thrown just six pitches. Ravenna 1, Malden 1.

Back in the dugout, Liam and Phillip sat at opposite ends of the bench. Liam sensed Phillip looking at him at one point, but when he turned his head, the pitcher looked away.

Four of Ravenna's batters got up in the bottom of the third. Matt grounded out, but Rodney got on base with a double. Liam hoped to start a rally with a crushing hit of his own, but he popped out. Mason struck out to end their chances. Neither Malden nor Forest Park crossed home plate in the fourth, so going into the top of the fifth, the board still showed them with a single run apiece.

Coach Driscoll conferred with his assistant coaches before Ravenna headed to the field. They made some substitutions, but to Liam's surprise and delight, he was still in the game. So was Phillip.

Guess we must be doing something right, Liam thought as he located his mitt.

Malden was at the bottom of its order. The hitter didn't look particularly strong, but Liam knew looks could be deceiving. Sure enough, he sent Phillip's first pitch toward third base. James Thrasher, in for Cole, jumped to make the catch. He was one of the taller players on Ravenna's roster, but he would have needed a six-inch vertical leap to land the ball in his glove. By the time Luis, now playing left field, scooped up the ball, the batter was standing safely at first.

James slapped his glove against his thigh, clearly disgusted with himself. Liam wanted to yell something encouraging to him. But he hesitated, remembering how Phillip felt about chatter. When James scuffed his cleat through the dirt, though, Liam decided the third baseman needed noise more than Phillip needed quiet.

"It's all right, it's all right, shake it off, Thrasher!" he called. He pounded his fist into his mitt. "Here we go, Ravenna, play is to first or second! Or better yet—first *and* second!"

The comment brought laughter from the stands. More important, it made James smile. When Tony slugged a bouncing grounder toward third, James was ready. He snared the ball on a hop and relayed it to Matt at second. One out—and then Matt whirled and hurled a pinpoint throw to Mason at first for out number two!

"Yes!" Liam celebrated the double play with a quick fist-pull by his side.

The celebration was short-lived, however. After throwing well for most of the game, Phillip gave up his first walk.

Ed, one of the three Malden players Liam had met, came up to bat. Sam had said Ed was a threat at the plate, but, so far, Liam hadn't seen much from him.

He should have paid closer attention.

CHAPTER
FOURTEEN

*G*TG, Carter texted Sean hurriedly. *My game's on.*

Carter and his Forest Park teammates had been cheering for Ravenna's double play when there was a loud knock on the hotel door. Ash opened it to find Coach Harrison and Coach Filbert on the other side.

"Nice to find you all together," Mr. Harrison said, looking amused. "Now stash all your electronics in your rooms and get yourselves in gear. The sun's out, the fields are drying, and we're due to play Calder in less than two hours."

There was a mad scramble as the boys hurried off to their own rooms to change. Carter and Ash took turns in the bathroom. Carter had just enough time to send the text to Sean before racing to join his teammates.

The earlier thunderstorm had whisked away the humidity that had hung over the ballpark for much of the tournament. The temperatures were in the high seventies when the game began. But without the oppressive mugginess, the air felt fresh and clean.

On the mound, Carter closed his eyes, took a deep lungful of that air, held it, and then let it out slowly. When he opened his eyes, he felt focused and ready to face Larry Miller, the first Calder batter.

Three pitches later, Larry returned to the dugout with his bat dragging behind him. Jarvis Greenaway took Larry's place in the batter's box. Carter mowed him down with three straight pitches, too. Calder's third batter fared no better.

Three up, three down.

A murmur of excitement rippled through the fans as Carter passed them on his way to the dugout. He suspected they were whispering about him, but he paid no attention. He was too busy thinking about the next batter he'd face: Ricky Muldoon.

Carter had struck Ricky out in the previous Forest Park–Calder game. Later that same game, however, Ricky had homered off Peter Molina. And in Calder's huge win over Groveland, the slugger had chalked up two more home runs and a stand-up double. Carter knew Ricky would pose a very dangerous threat.

Coach Harrison apparently agreed. He pulled Carter and Ash aside in the dugout and said, "Okay, we all know Muldoon has the power to send a pitch he likes over the fence. So"—he gave a devilish grin—"let's be sure he doesn't see something he likes."

Carter's eyes lit up. "You mean—the knuckleball?"

The coach nodded.

"Yes!" Carter high-fived Ash.

"I can't wait to see his face," Ash said, rubbing his hands together like a cartoon villain.

He didn't have to wait long, unfortunately, because Forest Park didn't do much its turn at bat. Of the four batters who went to the plate, only one singled. The others made outs.

Here we go. Carter tingled with anticipation as he watched Ricky assume his stance. He met the boy's narrow-eyed stare with equal intensity.

Ash flashed the signal for the knuckleball. Carter nodded, took a deep breath, and visualized the pitch in flight. Then he reared back and threw.

The ball traveled to the plate exactly as he had imagined it, bobbling up and down as it sped in. Ricky swatted at it but missed by a mile. Carter almost laughed out loud at the bewilderment he saw on the batter's face.

Strike one was followed by strikes two and three. Ricky stomped back to the dugout, his expression stormy.

The next Calder batter connected for a weak grounder that shortstop Allen Avery sent to Stephen Kline at first for another out. The sixth batter in Calder's lineup ticked two fouls down the third-base line. Raj tried for both but couldn't reach either in time.

Carter threw the same pitch again, hoping that if the ball went to the same spot, Raj could get it. This time, though, the ball arced up and looked good to drop fair.

"Mine!"

Ash tossed off his helmet and, mitt held high and open, raced to get under it. But instead of landing in his glove, the ball struck the mitt's fingertips and rolled off. Other players might have let it hit the ground. Not Ash. With catlike reflexes, he snatched the ball in his bare hand before it landed.

"Yer out!" the umpire yelled with a fierce slash of his fist.

The fans went crazy as Ash got to his feet, the ball still in his hand.

"That was amazing!" Carter crowed in the dugout. He was so thrilled for Ash that for a moment he forgot what the catch meant for him. If the ball had landed fair and the runner had reached base, his no-hitter would have been through.

He caught Ash's eye and sent him a silent thank-you. Ash, beaming, nodded in reply.

And Ash wasn't through yet. Up first for Forest Park, he practically tore the cover off the baseball with an over-the fence home run!

"Dude, you *own* this game!" Raj cried.

Ash laughed and then pointed to Carter. "Now it's your turn."

Carter chose a bat and approached the plate. He didn't homer, but he did get a respectable single. Raj, up next, did his duty with a sacrifice bunt that landed Carter safely at second. If Raj was disappointed not to get on base himself, he didn't show it. Instead, he gave an exaggerated shrug that seemed to say, "Eh, it's all for a good cause."

"Come on, Allen, hit me home, hit me home!" Carter yelled as the Forest Park shortstop stepped into the box. But Allen grounded out.

"Still alive out here, Charlie S.," Carter informed the next batter through cupped hands. Charlie kept him that way with a single between first and second. But when Stephen popped out, Carter and Charlie were left on base. Forest Park 1, Calder 0.

That was the score after Calder's turn at bat, too. Once again, Carter picked the opponents apart and sent them back to the dugout in order. Three innings pitched. Nine batters retired. No hits.

I'm halfway there, Carter thought. *And this time, I want to finish what I started!*

But would Coach Harrison keep him in for the full six innings? *He might,* Carter realized with a start, *if we stay on top.*

If Forest Park won today, the team wouldn't play again until the State tournament. That was five days away. Even if Carter threw the eighty-five pitches allowed in a single game by Little League, he could still pitch that first game, for he would have had the required four days' rest.

He shook his head. *Slow down, Jones, you're getting way ahead of yourself, thinking about States already! Who do you think you are—Liam?*

CHAPTER
FIFTEEN

*P*ow!

Oh, no.

Liam's heart leaped into his throat. After blasting three pitches wide of the first-base line, Ed laced Phillip's fourth pitch into deep right field. Rodney tore after it but couldn't reach the ball before it hit the ground.

Meanwhile, the runners were in motion. Ed pounded down the base path to first. The runner on first raced to second. Both touched the bags and kept going.

Liam was on his feet now, every muscle taut and ready. He had one eye on the runners, the other on his teammates. One part of his brain noted that Phillip had run behind the plate to back him up. The rest were screaming for Rodney to nab the ball and get it to Matt, the cutoff man, faster, *faster*, before it was too late!

Rodney picked up the ball. As he whirled and threw to Matt, the lead runner hit third and Ed touched second. Neither slowed his step.

Whap! The ball socked into Matt's glove. He spun around, ball in hand, and hesitated for a split second.

"Here! *Here!*" Liam bellowed even as Coach Driscoll yelled for Matt to throw to home. The lead runner was bearing down like a runaway locomotive, but Liam was sure he could tag him out if only Matt would throw him the ball!

And then the unthinkable happened: Matt threw, but his throw was wild!

Liam knew he could never make the catch. If he tried, he'd be out of position for the tag. There was only one way Ravenna could stop Malden from scoring and that was if—

"Liam!"

Phillip had scooped up the ball. Liam twisted around to catch it. It struck his glove just as the runner hit the dirt for a feet-first slide. Liam whirled back, swept his glove down, and brushed the runner's leg.

But even as he made the tag, he knew he was too late. The runner had already crossed the plate.

The umpire confirmed it. "Safe!" he called, fanning his arms out to either side.

The Malden runner leaped to his feet and punched the air once before rushing back to the dugout. There, his overjoyed teammates flocked around him, slapping him on the back and socking him in the shoulder. The boy himself was grinning so widely Liam thought his cheeks must hurt.

"We almost had him."

Liam started. He'd forgotten that Phillip was standing there. Before he could react, though, Phillip headed back to the mound.

Malden now had a one-run lead, but that was all it got that inning. Ed was left stranded on base when Phillip mowed down Sam on three straight pitches.

In the dugout, Coach Driscoll talked briefly to Matt before nodding him to the bench. Liam knew the coach was trying to cheer him up after the wild throw, but it didn't work. Matt plopped down like the weight of the world was on his shoulders.

"Sorry, guys," he mumbled. "That run was all my fault."

No one said a word. Then Phillip snorted and shook his head. "You know what, Matt?"

Liam exchanged an uneasy glance with Rodney.

Rodney cleared his throat. "Hey, Phillip, maybe you should—"

"That run *was* someone's fault," Phillip continued as if Rodney hadn't spoken. "But it wasn't yours. It was mine. That runner wouldn't have been on base if I hadn't walked him."

"Well, if we're pointing fingers," Rodney piped in, "we better stick one in my face, too. That batter clocked three powerful fouls to the right. I should have moved back in case he straightened one out."

"It was my job to warn you," Liam objected.

Matt lifted a shoulder and let it drop. "Thanks, guys, really, but—"

"This is a team," Phillip said firmly. "No one person wins or loses games."

Finally, Matt cracked a smile. "Yeah, okay. You're right."

"'Course he is," Rodney said. "Now leave the last inning behind you and get ready. You're up third."

"And I'm up first." Christopher Frost jumped up, stuck a helmet on his head, and trotted out to the plate. A pale boy with glasses and a perpetually sunburned nose, he had a habit of waggling his bony hips while waiting for the pitch. Unfortunately, the waggle didn't translate into power. Christopher popped out to the catcher.

Phillip, up next, fared better. He watched one pitch sail by for a strike and a second for a ball, but he sent the third skipping through the gap between first and second for a single. Matt followed Phillip. The pep talk from his teammates must have done him good, for he hit the ball to shallow left field.

"Go! Go! Go!" Liam and the others yelled. And then, "Yes!" because Phillip had reached third and Matt stood safe and sound at second.

"My turn!" Rodney chose his favorite bat and took his place in the box. A confident hitter, he made the players on the bench laugh with his perfect imitation of Christopher's hip waggle.

"Aw, I don't look like that," Christopher protested with a good-natured grin. "Do I?"

Rodney socked a single. Phillip and Matt were forced to stay where they were. Bases loaded, one out, and—

"Liam, you're up," Dr. Driscoll called.

Liam's mouth suddenly turned dry. He'd been so busy watching the game he'd forgotten he followed Rodney in the batting order. Now he licked his lips and walked toward the batter's box, twisting his gloved hands on the bat's handle and swallowing hard.

The crowd fell silent. The Malden pitcher leaned forward, ball behind his back, and stared down from the mound.

No doubt the stare was meant to intimidate. But Liam thought he detected something hiding behind the steely gaze.

He's worried.

That thought gave him a little jolt of confidence. When the first pitch came, he swung hard. *Crack!*

It wasn't the crushing homer he'd hoped for, but a line drive single that ripped past the pitcher into center field. The Ravenna runners flew around the bases, with Phillip crossing home plate to tie the score at two runs each.

Ravenna's fans went crazy, stomping, clapping, and cheering. Liam saw Melanie's camera trained on him, and while he knew it wasn't cool, he couldn't help grinning and giving a thumbs-up.

Malden changed pitchers after that. The reliever struck out Mason. James was up next.

Come on, man, don't leave us hanging out here, Liam thought as his skinny teammate stepped into the box.

James popped a pitch into the space between the

shortstop and the pitcher. It should have been an easy out. But the pitcher backpedaled just as the shortstop lunged forward. They collided with such force that both fell!

"Run!" Ravenna's first-base coach screamed.

CHAPTER SIXTEEN

I told you you owned this game!"

Raj pounded Ash on the back. The catcher had just clocked an RBI double that scored Luke from third and gave Forest Park its second run. Unfortunately, Carter ended the inning by grounding out.

He redeemed himself in the top of the fourth, however, by plucking a screaming line drive out of the air. He let out a sigh of relief when he saw the ball nestled securely in his glove. Had he missed, that blast would definitely have been a hit—and his no-hitter would have been done.

Not that preserving the no-hitter was his main goal. His focus was, and would always be, on winning the game. Still, he couldn't kid himself that posting six no-hit innings would make a victory much sweeter.

It wasn't until he was sitting in the dugout that something suddenly occurred to him. So far, each inning he'd pitched had been a three-up, three-down effort. He wasn't closing in on a no-hitter; he was closing in on a perfect game!

Don't think about it. Don't think about it. Don't think about it. Just when he thought his mind might explode, he remembered Rachel's book. He grabbed it out of his duffel bag the way a starving man would grab a piece of bread.

The joke he read was as lame as ever—*Q: Why was Cinderella so bad at baseball? A: Because she had a pumpkin for a coach!*—but Carter laughed out loud at the illustration. It showed Rachel as the princess and Coach Harrison as a pumpkin with a baseball hat. Silly, but it helped loosen the tension that had gripped his innards.

Raj started things off with a double. Allen followed with a single. Ron, now in for Charlie Santiago, singled as well to load the bases.

Calder called time then to make a pitching change. Carter wasn't surprised. The pitcher had given up ten hits so far, including two doubles and a home run with two runs earned. He walked slowly off the mound, his coach's arm around his shoulder.

The new pitcher was a southpaw. His fastball confounded Freddie and Keith. Both struck out. Back in the dugout, they sat next to each other, lending truth to the phrase "misery loves company."

Craig chose his bat. Earlier in the game, he'd been caught off base, turning what should have been a single out into a double play for Calder. Now he strode to the plate with fire in his eyes and ripped the first pitch between first and second. The runners tore up the base paths. Raj crossed home plate standing up.

"Yes!"

Carter, Ash, and the other boys on the bench leaped up, pounding their hands together as Raj jogged into the dugout. Freddie clapped the scrawny third baseman on the back so hard that Raj stumbled. But he never stopped smiling.

Peter, in for Charlie Murray, was all smiles, too, after reaching first on a mishandled grounder. Allen dashed home on that same error to make the score Forest Park 4, Calder 0. Bases were still loaded with Ron at third, Craig at second, and Peter at first.

Ash took a deep breath. "My turn. Wish me luck," he

said as he put on a batting helmet. "No, wait. Wish me skill!"

"Skill!" the boys on the bench chorused together.

"Bring 'em home, LaBrie!" Carter added as Ash stepped into the batter's box.

Ash hefted the bat over his shoulder, poised and ready. The first pitch came. Ash let it go by.

"Ball!"

Two more pitches, one a strike and the other a ball. Ash stepped out, tapped the bat against his cleats, glanced up at the pitcher, and then moved back into place again.

Carter leaned forward. "Come on, Ash, you can do it," he murmured.

Another pitch. Another strike. The count was two-and-two. Then—*pow!* Ash swung with such power Carter was amazed the bat didn't splinter. The ball vanished into the clear blue sky and fell just inside the fence, where it bounced away from the center fielder's desperate grasp.

"Holy moley!" Freddie cried.

"Holy moley shlamoley!" Raj one-upped him.

"It's a triple!" they said together.

Ron scored standing up. So did Craig. When Peter slid under the catcher's tag, Forest Park's score jumped to seven runs!

Carter continued the rally with a single. Ash wisely stayed put at third. When Raj came up to bat, Carter realized that Forest Park had run through its entire batting order that inning. That was as far down the list as it got, however. Raj struck out.

Ash had barely ducked beneath the overhang when his teammates swarmed him.

"That was unbelievable!"

"Incredible hit, man, incredible!"

"You been holding out on us? Since when do you crush the ball like that?"

"Guys, guys," Ash said, grinning. "I've got to put on my gear. Or did you forget we've got two innings to go? Carter, help me out here!"

Carter handed him his helmet. As he did, Ash locked eyes with him. "I've had my highlight moment," he said. "Now let's get you yours."

He held up a fist. Carter raised his eyebrows. He made a fist, too, but instead of bumping Ash's with his knuckles, he hammered it down, then up, then down again. "Let's go."

Ricky Muldoon led off the top of the fifth. He'd been baffled by Carter's knuckleball earlier, but that didn't mean he wasn't a threat. Ash stood up and waved the outfield back.

It was a good thing he did because Ricky belted Carter's first pitch with all his strength!

Carter spun around—and sagged with disappointment. The ball was soaring to the back fence, just to the left of the spot where Ash's triple had flown minutes earlier. Center fielder Ron Davis was on the move, but Carter knew he'd never get under the ball in time.

Oh, well, he thought. He started turning back. Then he heard the crowd collectively gasp. He whirled around just in time to see Peter Molina, racing across from left field, soar higher than seemed humanly possible and capture the ball!

Hold on to it, hold on to it, hold on to it, Carter pleaded silently.

Peter fell to the ground, and then rolled over, jumped up, and triumphantly showed everyone that the ball was still stuck in his glove.

"Yer out!" the umpire cried.

"No!"

Enraged, Ricky kicked the dirt beside the plate with such force he left a gouge mark. The umpire barked out a caution, but Ricky seemed beyond caring. He stormed off the field and flung himself onto the bench. Calder's assistant coach was beside him immediately. Ricky shook him off angrily but then put his face in his hands and let the man sit beside him.

The inning ended mercifully soon after that, with a groundout and a strikeout. The Forest Park players moved quickly and quietly off the field, subdued by Ricky's outburst. They found their voices in the dugout, however, and were generous with their praise for Peter's outstanding catch.

Peter caught Carter's eye. "No way I was letting that go for a hit," he said firmly. "Nope. No way."

Carter didn't say anything. But his heart was hammering a staccato drumbeat. *One more inning. If we can keep them off base for just one more inning...* He refused to finish the thought.

CHAPTER
SEVENTEEN

Run!"

The shout from the first-base coach was unnec-
essary. Liam had anticipated the collision between
Malden's pitcher and shortstop a split second before
it happened. He'd already taken off when the two col-
lapsed into a heap, the baseball rolling away from them
in the grass.

Now he was thirty feet from second and picking
up speed. The pitcher and shortstop untangled themselves and jumped up. Liam was twenty feet away when
the player covering the bag started yelling for the ball.
Ten feet when the shortstop scrambled forward to get

it. Five feet when he picked it up. Three feet when he tossed it to second.

Liam hit the dirt. But instead of sliding straight, he aimed his outstretched foot away from the bag and reached to touch the base with his left hand. When the Malden player swept his glove down for the tag, Liam instinctively yanked his hand away—and then flipped over to slap the bag with his right!

"Safe!" the umpire cried.

The fans went crazy—and their cheers grew louder when Matt, making the most of the catching error, crossed home plate. Ravenna 3, Malden 2.

"Okay, Carmen, sweeten that lead for us!" Liam heard Sean yell above the din of the crowd.

But Carmen grounded out.

Liam jogged off second base. He was happy to have helped the team leapfrog ahead of Malden, but he would have been happier if the gap were wider.

It was the top of the sixth inning, Malden's last chance to score. With the Sectional title on the line, the batters would no doubt be giving one hundred and ten percent.

So we'll have to give one hundred and twenty, he thought as he suited up in his catcher's gear. *Or even better—*

"Hey, Liam."

Liam looked up to see Phillip standing beside him.

"I just had a great idea," the pitcher said. "How about we win this tourney here and now by sending Malden's batters packing one"—Phillip touched a finger to his chest—"two"—he brushed that same finger against the tip of his nose—"three." He pointed at Liam.

Liam stared at Phillip. Then he broke into a slow smile.

To most anyone else, the chest-nose-point gesture would have been meaningless. To Liam, it symbolized the heart of their rocky relationship.

He'd used it on Phillip first and as a prank—sort of. At last year's World Series, Liam had learned about the practical joke Phillip had played on Carter during baseball camp. When Liam encountered Phillip shortly afterward, he'd decided to return the favor with a trick of his own. He pointed to a nonexistent stain on Phillip's shirt. When Phillip automatically looked down to see the stain for himself, Liam jerked his finger up and bopped him in the nose, crowing, "Made you look!"

Phillip had the last laugh, however. After he struck Liam out, he leaned over Liam, imitated the nose-bop, and whispered, "Made you whiff!"

He'd repeated the gesture throughout the regular season, whenever he and Liam faced each other on the field. Seeing it always made Liam's blood boil, for he knew it was meant to remind him of his humiliating strikeout and therefore to undermine his confidence.

But he knew that wasn't Phillip's intention now. Now, Phillip was using the gesture to forge a new bond between them—a bond of trust.

Liam stood up. Still smiling, he pointed to his own chest, then his nose, and then pointed at Phillip. "One. Two. Three," he said in sync with each movement. "Sounds good to me. Let's do it."

Then he curled his finger back and held out his fist. Phillip did the same. "One, two, three," they said together as they bumped knuckles.

Agreeing to put the batters down in order was one thing; actually doing it was another. And yet Liam felt more confident than he had all game. Phillip appeared more determined, too.

Zip! Swish! Thud! Zip! Swish! Thud! Zip! Swish! Thud! Three screaming fastballs translated into three strikes and out number one.

"Two to go, two to go!" Liam cried as he sent the ball to third for the start of a trip around the horn.

Back in his squat, he sized up the batter. The Malden player was a substitute taking his first turn at bat that game, but Liam remembered him from their previ-

122

ous meeting. He hadn't been a threat then—and he was no match for Phillip's changeup now. He reached for the first two and missed. He connected on the third but only for a pop-up toward shortstop. Christopher caught it for out number two.

The people in the stands buzzed with excitement as the ball whipped around the bases again. Then they fell silent, as if holding their collective breath, when the third Malden batter walked to the plate.

As the boy tapped the dirt from his cleats, Liam caught a glimpse of his face. He looked nervous. No, more than nervous: petrified. Liam felt a wave of pity for him and nearly murmured a word of encouragement. Then the boy stepped into the box and the urge vanished.

They were in competition for the title, after all.

From the mound, Phillip gave the batter a steely-eyed stare. Then he nodded at Liam's signal for a changeup. After using his arm to wipe sweat from his forehead, he reared back and threw.

Crack! The ball rocketed into the air behind first base. For a split second, the boy just stood there, open-mouthed with astonishment. Then he dropped the bat and ran to first.

"Go! Go! Go!" his teammates screamed.

He's fast, Liam saw with a sinking heart. *He'll beat the throw.*

In right field, Rodney made a valiant dive for the ball, but it fell out of reach. The Malden boy touched first, spotted Rodney sprawled in the grass, and took off for second.

Bad idea! Liam thought. He was right.

Rodney sprang to his feet, snagging the ball as he did, and turned to throw to Matt at second. As fast as the Malden player was, there was no way he could out-run a speeding baseball. Even if Matt missed, Phillip was right there backing him up.

Matt didn't miss. Foot firmly on the bag, he caught the ball and nailed the runner with the tag.

The umpire yelled the words Liam and his team-mates had longed to hear: "Yer out!"

CHAPTER
EIGHTEEN

One walk. That's all it took for Carter's perfect game to vanish like water through a sieve. Disappointment swept over him as he watched the batter toss the bat aside and trot to first base.

Ash called time and jogged to the mound. He placed the baseball in Carter's glove and then stared him in the eye. "Forget about it. Focus on the next batter. Be on the lookout for the bunt. And keep one eye on the runner, too," he added. "He's fast. His coach might have him try for second."

Carter glanced at the boy on first, bit his lip, and nodded.

"Not that he'd get there safely," Ash said

matter-of-factly. "I'd make the throw. Freddie would make the catch. He'd be out before he even had a chance to hit the slide."

"Let's go, boys!" the umpire called.

As it turned out, both of Ash's predictions for what might happen came true. When Carter released the ball, the batter squared off for a bunt and the runner took off for second. But the bunt misfired, popping the ball up a few feet instead of sending it straight down. Ash lunged forward and nabbed it for the out.

The runner faltered midway down the base path. Carter could almost hear his frantic thought: *Go back to first or continue to second?*

He kept going. Ash heaved the ball to Freddie. The runner didn't stand a chance; Freddie barely had to move to make the catch. He swept his glove down for the tag. The runner was out. Double play!

Any fight left in Calder's players evaporated in that instant. The third batter swung at three pitches. He missed each one.

Final score: Forest Park 7, Calder 0.

The fans applauded like mad for both teams, shouting congratulations to their favorite players. Carter barely heard them.

"I did it," he whispered. "I pitched a no-hitter." Then

he gazed at his teammates and grinned at his foolish statement. "No, I didn't do it. *We* did." He ran off the mound to join them.

He'd only gone a few steps when someone hurtled onto the field, grabbed him in a bear hug, and whirled him around. "You were amazing!"

"Rachel?" Carter disentangled himself from her grasp. "I thought you were back home! How'd you get here? *When* did you get here?"

"Nice to see you, too," she said drily. "I got here just as the game started. Mrs. LaBrie brought me."

"Ash's mom? I didn't know she was going to be here."

Rachel grinned. "Neither did he. Look." She jutted her chin toward the stands.

Carter spotted his friend in the crowd just as Ash's mother found him. The look of pure delight on Ash's face when he saw her made Carter's heart glow.

"Hang on," he said suddenly. He turned to her with an accusing eye. "No way you were here the whole game. I would have heard you yelling."

Rachel made a face. "Mrs. LaBrie wouldn't let me. She was afraid Ash would look over and see her and that it would throw him off his game. But I can yell all I want now!"

With that, she threw her head back and bellowed to

the sky, "Woo-hoo! Forest Park is going to States! Phew," she added in her normal voice. "Now come on, let's go get Ash. I want to hug him, too."

"You go," Carter said. "I want to see my parents."

But when he looked for them, he found only his mother. His father, it turned out, was the reason Mrs. LaBrie was at the game. "He called her this morning and offered to cover the Diamond Champs so she could be here," his mother said.

"Oh." Carter tried to hide his disappointment that his dad hadn't seen his no-hitter.

Mrs. Jones saw right through him, though. She brushed his hair off his forehead and gazed at him with her soft, warm eyes. "He'll be bummed, too," she murmured. "But he realized how badly Ash's mom wanted to be here. Isn't it nice that you both had a parent to see your triumph?"

Carter nodded and then laughed. "Well, she couldn't have seen a better game, huh? Ash was phenomenal!"

"He was," she agreed. "And so were you." She took his hand and gave it a squeeze.

The rest of the day passed in a blur. Forest Park had its official team photo taken, and then parents insisted on taking dozens more of individual players, players in pairs, and players in groups. Mrs. LaBrie and Mrs. Jones must have snapped at least a hundred of Carter and Ash together.

"There's one for the wall," Carter's mother said, showing one of the grinning boys with their arms around each other's shoulders.

Finally, the players were allowed to head for home. Because Mr. Jones had taken their car, Carter, Ash, Rachel, and Mrs. Jones all got a ride with Mrs. LaBrie. Carter sent Liam a quick text to let him know they'd won and that he'd be in touch in the morning. He wasn't sure if it went through, though, because the signal was poor. After waiting a minute for a reply, he turned off his phone and put it away.

They stopped just once, to pick up some take-out burgers—or "nasty road food," as Mrs. Jones called it— but still the sun had long since gone down by the time they dropped Rachel at her house.

"Not sure I'll be able to make States," she said regretfully.

"Hey, if not, at least your lame-o jokes will," Carter replied. He patted the pocket of his duffel bag where he kept her little book. She flashed her one-hundred-watt grin and then hurried into her house, ponytail swinging behind her.

Ten minutes later, Mrs. LaBrie pulled into her driveway. Carter and his mother said their good-byes and walked the short distance to their own house.

Mr. Jones met them at the door. "Welcome home, champ!" He folded Carter into a huge hug.

Just then, someone in the driveway cleared his throat. It was Ash. "Uh, Carter, your mom forgot this in our car." He handed Carter a pair of women's sunglasses, mumbled a good night, and left.

Carter watched him go and then looked up at his father. "Dad, can I ask you something? Do you know anything about Ash's father?"

Mr. Jones shook his head. "I don't. But your mother might. You could ask her. Shower first, though, okay?"

Mrs. Jones was already in bed asleep when Carter finished in the bathroom. He tiptoed in, laid her sunglasses on her bedside table, and crept out.

It was after eleven o'clock when he finally climbed into bed. Before he turned out his light, he checked his phone for messages. There was one from Sean and one from Liam. He smiled when he read them, for they both said the same thing: "We won!"

CHAPTER NINETEEN

Liam had hoped to video-chat with Carter after his win but remembered his cousin had a much longer drive home from his tournament than he had. He left his laptop on in case a call did come through and then went downstairs to watch a movie with his parents. It was a boring film, all about some historic event he knew nothing about, so after half an hour he decided to just go to bed.

He didn't fall asleep but rather lay with his hands laced behind his head, thinking about everything that had happened since the game.

Sam Witherspoon caught up with him immediately after the congratulatory hand-slap.

"I thought we had you beat," Sam confessed. "When DiMaggio gave up that walk and RBI triple just before I came to the plate, I thought, 'This is it. He's going down.'" He shook his head ruefully. "Even after I got out, I still thought we could pick him apart in the sixth. Truth is, I could have sworn there was friction between you two. I thought we'd be able to use that against you. But when you guys took the field, I don't know. Something seemed...different."

He looked so puzzled that Liam couldn't help laughing. "Something was different," he told Sam. "Phillip and I finally stopped *pretending* we were teammates and actually started *being* teammates."

Sam snorted. "You couldn't have waited until after today's game for that to happen?"

"What can I say?" Liam spread his hands wide. "The time was right."

Sam pointed a finger at Liam. "You're a good guy, McGrath. In fact, I've got a hunch that you're going to make it all the way back to Williamsport. And I'll be cheering for you the whole way."

"Thanks, man." The two shook hands and then Liam left to rejoin his teammates.

"There you are!" Rodney cried when he spotted him. "Time for the team photo. Oh, and I nabbed you one of these. Here." He gave Liam a commemorative trading pin designed especially for their Sectional tournament and watched while Liam attached it to his jersey. "Now come on, there's like a zillion people waiting to take our picture!"

"And one sister waiting for a postgame interview."

Liam turned to find Melanie hurrying toward him, a huge smile on her face. She handed her video camera to Rodney. "Get this on film, will you?" Then she took Liam by the shoulders and stared him in the eye. "Okay, bro, listen up because I don't say this very often. Ready? I'm really proud of you."

Liam put his hand to his chest and staggered back in mock amazement. "Rodney, please tell me you got that!"

"Every word, my friend!"

"Give me that," Melanie groused as she took the camera back from Rodney. "Now, about that interview—?"

"Rodney! Liam! We're waiting!" Dr. Driscoll called from the far side of the field.

"Sorry, Mel, gotta go! But I promise I'll let you interview me tomorrow!"

There weren't a zillion people poised with cameras, just one official Little League photographer. She instructed the boys to line up behind the championship banner. They arranged themselves as they had for the District Championship photo, with one big exception.

"Yo, McGrath, got a spot for you right here!" Phillip called.

When the camera flashed, Liam was standing shoulder-to-shoulder with Phillip, their hands joined and raised in victory.

After the photo, Dr. Driscoll rounded up his players and assistant coaches for a final wrap-up. "I wish there was some way for me to express just how pleased I am with what we accomplished this tournament," he began.

"There is!" Rodney cut in. "Take us out for pizza!"

Dr. Driscoll burst out laughing. "You know what? I think I will! Everybody, dinner's on me!"

Half an hour later, the Ravenna players and their families descended on Mario's, a local pizza restaurant. It was only four o'clock, too early for the dinner rush, so the place was empty. The boys got permission to push several tables together into one big row. Once the red-and-white-checked tablecloths were straightened, the waiters brought pitchers of soda, plastic tumblers filled with ice, and silverware wrapped in paper napkins. Steaming hot pizza loaded with pepperoni, cheese, sausage, and other toppings arrived shortly after.

"Now this is what I call a postgame meeting," Rodney said, surveying the spread with great satisfaction.

"Funny," Sean said, "I just call it food."

The party broke up soon after the pizza was gone. "I'll be in touch with details about the Sub-Division tourney," Coach Driscoll told the players' parents. One by one, the families left until only the Driscolls, the McGraths, and the DiMaggios remained.

That's when Melanie pounced. "You know, Phillip," she said, sidling up to the pitcher with a movie-star smile, "I've been trying to get an interview with you and Liam for a while. What do you say? How about tomorrow at one o'clock?"

Phillip agreed, but only if it was okay with Liam.

"Of course it is," Melanie answered for her brother. When Liam started to protest, she hit a button on her camera. Liam heard a playback of his voice say, "I promise I'll let you interview me tomorrow!"

"She's got you there, fella," Mr. McGrath said with a laugh. "One o'clock tomorrow it is!"

The three families headed to the restaurant door together then.

"Oh, Liam, before I forget, here." Sean fished around in his pocket and pulled out Liam's cell phone. "I texted Carter the play-by-play through the fifth inning. Then he had to get ready for his own game. Oh, and there are some photos of you during and after the game, too."

"Awesome. Thanks, man," Liam said. "I'll give him the rest of the details later."

"And find out if he's going to States, right?"

"You got it!"

"Carter?" Phillip asked. "Carter Jones?"

Liam nodded.

Phillip crossed his arms over his chest. "You still keep in touch with him?"

Liam gave a laugh. "Well, yeah! He's my cousin."

Phillip's eyes widened in disbelief. "He *is*?"

"You didn't know that?"

"No, I didn't. So you tell him everything that happens in our games?"

"Sure do."

Phillip shook his head but didn't say another word. When his father drove up, he climbed into the backseat. A moment later, they were gone.

The Driscolls and the McGraths parted to head to their own cars. Mrs. McGrath stood next to Liam while they waited for Mr. McGrath to open the doors.

"Hey," she said in a voice pitched softly so only he could hear it.

He looked up at her. The late afternoon sunlight

kissed her brown hair, turning it golden. She tucked a strand behind her ear and smiled. "It was nice seeing you and Phillip getting along so well."

He smiled back. "Yeah. Seems I found the words at the right time."

She reached forward and playfully tugged his cap over his eyes. "I always knew you would."

Liam dozed on the ride home, waking when the car bumped into the driveway and pulled to a stop. He unloaded his gear from the back and then went upstairs to take a shower.

"Give me your uniform so I can wash it," his mother called. He opened the bathroom door a crack, shoved his clothes out, and closed it again. He was just finishing his shower when he suddenly remembered the trading pin he'd attached to the uniform's collar. He raced downstairs just in time to remove it before his mother tossed the jersey into the wash. He carried the pin up to his room and set it on his bedside table. Then he went to his closet and found his pin bag.

Inside were dozens of pins he'd collected or traded for over the past few years. One row was made up of those he'd received after the Pennsylvania Little League Championships the summer before. Carter had duplicates of each in his own collection.

But he won't have this one, Liam suddenly thought, staring at his newest pin. *Or the one from Ravenna's District tourney. And I won't have any of the pins he gets after. Forest Park's tournaments.*

Now, lying in bed, Liam realized that wasn't exactly true. There was one pin they both might receive: the one given in August to the players who reached the Little League Baseball World Series.

CHAPTER
TWENTY

Aw, man, what time is it?" Liam asked groggily.

Carter was sitting on his front porch with his laptop in front of him. He glanced at the computer's clock. "Ten o'clock," he answered.

Liam scrubbed his face with his hands and groaned. "You dork! That means it's seven o'clock here. I was sound asleep!"

Carter laughed. "I wouldn't have called except I saw you were online. Sorry if I woke you up."

"No, you're not."

"Yeah, I'm not."

Liam peered at him. "What are you eating?"

Carter held up a chocolate-glazed doughnut. Liam

groaned again. "Tell me that's not from Hendrick's!" he whined plaintively, naming his favorite bakery in Pennsylvania.

"I would, but then I'd be lying." He leaned forward and took a big bite. "Mmmm, this is the best doughnut in the world."

"I hate you," Liam said. Then he told Carter to hang on so he could get his own breakfast. When he reappeared, he looked grumpy. "No doughnuts, no bagels, no nothing good, so guess what I'm having for breakfast?" He lifted up a spoon filled with brown flakes of cereal. "Bran. And it's already turning to wallpaper paste."

He tilted the spoon slowly. Carter heard a *plop* as the mushy lump hit the bowl. He grimaced and put his doughnut aside. "Appetite gone, thanks."

"Serves you right. Now you can tell me about your game without a mouth full of food. I know you won."

Carter leaned back and assumed a posture of nonchalance. "Oh, let's see. I threw a no-hitter and—"

"What!?" Liam exclaimed. "No way!"

"Way!"

"No!"

"Yes—hang on, why is that so hard for you to believe?"

140

Liam cracked up. "Not hard to believe—unbelievable! Congrats, dork, really. Now, give me the details."

Carter told him everything. When he came to Peter's amazing catch, Liam pointed a finger at him. "You tell Peter that Liam says he's the man."

"He was," Carter agreed. "And you should have seen Ash!" He started listing off everything the catcher had done—his home run, his triple, the crucial double play in the final inning. After a moment, though, Liam cut him off.

"Yeah, yeah, yeah, blah, blah, blah, enough about Forest Park already!" Liam cut in. "Aren't you going to ask about my game?"

"Fine," Carter said, rolling his eyes. "I know most of what happened thanks to Sean. But tell me how it ended."

The tone of Liam's voice changed then, from joking to wonderment. "It ended with Phillip and me as friends. Look." He fumbled for his cell phone, hit a few buttons, and then held it up for Carter to see. "Sean took this."

Carter found himself staring at a picture of Liam and Phillip, fists touching and wide grins on their faces. If he hadn't seen it for himself, he would never have believed it was real—or would have assumed the picture had been edited. As it was, the image hit him like a punch in the gut.

"How?" he managed to ask. "Last I knew, he was driving you up the wall."

Liam shook his head as if bewildered and then told Carter about his rant. "I think I hit a nerve or something. I don't know. I guess I can ask him later. He's coming here so Melanie can interview us together."

"Oh. That's nice." Carter tried but failed to keep sarcasm from creeping into his tone.

"Carter—"

"Sorry, sorry. It's just, you know. *Phillip.*" He shook his head. "It's going to take me awhile to wrap my head around you getting along with him." He scrunched up his eyes in concentration and then opened them. "Okay, there. Done."

Liam held his fist up to the screen. "States, dork."

"Southern California South Sub-Divisionals, doofus." They both cracked up at the tournament's long title and then said their good-byes. Before they signed off, Carter punched his screen in time with Liam's taps. Then Liam's image was replaced with an automated video-chat message.

Call ended, the message read.

Carter logged off, closed his laptop, and tucked it

under his arm. As he stood to go inside, he noticed his half-eaten doughnut on the paper napkin where he'd left it. He wadded it up, carried it to the kitchen, and threw it away.

Suddenly antsy, Carter went up to his room, wondering what to do with his free time. Lucky Boy seemed to have an idea. The black-and-tan dog rescued the pink rubber ball from under the bunk beds and dropped it at Carter's feet with a hopeful bark.

But Coach Harrison had cautioned him to give his arm a complete rest—"Not even a game of fetch with that dog of yours!"—so Carter ignored the ball and went to get Lucky Boy's leash from the hallway instead.

There he saw his mother had already hung the photo of him arm in arm with Ash. He stared at it for a long moment and then whistled for Lucky Boy.

"Come on, fella, let's go to the hideout."

The hideout was Liam and Carter's secret place. Hidden deep in the woods behind their houses, it was a natural shelter made of boulders and surrounded by brush and trees. The cousins had discovered it when they were younger. They'd made a solemn vow never to share its location with anyone else. True to his word, Carter had visited it a few times since Liam had moved but always on his own.

Until now. He met up with Ash by chance at the start of his walk. Before, he would have turned away from the path in the woods. This time, he headed straight for it with Ash and Lucky Boy in tow.

Ash had known for a long time that Carter had something secret hidden in the woods. He'd tried to persuade Carter to tell him what it was but dropped the questions when Carter evaded them. Now he shot Carter a surprised look but didn't say anything.

It took fifteen minutes to reach the shelter. Carter knelt down, crawled inside, and came out dragging the green plastic bin he and Liam had stashed there long ago. Inside the bin were a few old beach towels and some flashlights. He spread out one towel, gave Ash another, and sat down.

After a moment's hesitation, Ash sat beside him. "So," he said. "This is the secret you've been hiding, huh?"

Carter let Lucky Boy off his leash before answering. Then he told Ash the story of how he and Liam found it. "It's where I go when I need to think," he finished.

Ash surveyed the shelter appreciatively. "I can see why. Thanks for showing it to me."

Carter was glad he didn't ask why he'd revealed the

hideout after keeping it secret for so long. He wasn't sure how he'd answer.

"Do your parents know about this place? Your dad?" Ash asked suddenly.

Carter looked at him sideways. "No. Why?"

Ash picked up a rock and threw it, watching as Lucky Boy bounded after it. "I don't know. You and your father seem so close, I just figured..." His voice trailed away.

Carter almost asked Ash about his own dad. The question was on the tip of his tongue. Then his cell phone chimed and the opportunity was lost.

"It's my mom," he said with a glance at the tiny screen. "We're supposed to go home right away. Our parents have something to tell us."

"What?" Ash asked.

Carter shook his head. "No clue, but we're supposed to hurry."

CHAPTER
TWENTY-ONE

Liam glanced at the clock. It read 1:32, two minutes later than when he'd last looked at it and thirty-two minutes past the time Melanie had scheduled the joint interview with Phillip.

Melanie paced back and forth through the living room. "Try calling him again."

Liam dialed the DiMaggios' home number. "Voice mail again," he said, holding the phone out so she could hear the recording. He hung up without leaving a message. He'd already left three, after all, so what was the point of another?

"I can't believe you don't have his cell number," Melanie fumed.

"Well, I don't," he answered peevishly. "I mean, come on, we barely talked to each other until yesterday, so why would I?"

She threw her hands up in the air and then flopped down in an oversize sofa chair. "Talk about a total bust. I—"

The doorbell rang.

"He's here!" Melanie sprang up to answer it. She returned looking put out. "It's just the Driscolls."

"Great to see you, too," Sean said, taking the seat she had vacated. He gestured to the video camera set up at one end of the room. "What's with that?"

Liam explained about the interview.

"Huh, that's weird," Rodney said. "We just saw Phillip and he didn't say anything about it."

"You saw him? Where?" Melanie asked eagerly.

"At the Bergs. We were all visiting Owen."

"Maybe he's going to come here afterward," Liam ventured.

"Doubt it," Sean said matter-of-factly. "He and Owen were about to watch a movie. A trilogy, actually. He didn't say anything about an interview." He gave a lazy stretch. "So, got anything to eat? How about a plate of nachos with melted cheese and salsa and a side of sour cream and that guacamole your mom always has in the fridge? I'll wait here while you make it."

Happy for an excuse to hide his disappointment, Liam went to the kitchen to fix Sean his snack. When he returned, he found the Driscolls and Melanie gathered around the television. Melanie had rigged up her camera to play videos on the big screen. She gave her brother a sly smile and opened a file marked "Bloopers: Liam."

Liam cringed, certain the clip would show him messing up during baseball games. Instead, he saw a compilation of him acting goofy—like when he answered her question with his mouth full of chewed-up bagel. She'd added voice-over commentary to some moments, which just made the video that much funnier.

"This is hilarious! Tell me Carter's seen it," Rodney said, wiping away tears of laughter.

"Tell me he hasn't!" Liam said.

"Not yet," Melanie teased.

"What else do you have?" Sean wanted to know.

Melanie scrolled through her file list. "No more bloopers, but I do have montages of each player."

"Montages, awesome," Sean said. Then after a pause he asked, "What's a montage?"

She laughed. "It's a bunch of different clips of a subject that flow into one another. Look, here's what I've got for Rodney so far."

She tapped an icon and Rodney's image appeared.

"Oooh, who *is* that handsome devil?" Rodney said, preening. "Look, there he is again! And again! And—ew, gross! What am I doing?"

The video showed him standing in the outfield and examining something in his armpit. Whatever it was seemed to fascinate him, because the clip went on for several seconds, much to Liam and Sean's delight. When it finally ended, they applauded.

"That'll end up on the cutting-room floor, right?" Rodney asked hopefully.

"If you're very, very nice to me," Melanie answered, "maybe."

The boys pestered her to share more montages, but she refused. "You'll have to wait for the movie," she said primly. "Now shoo. I got an idea while I was watching these and want to get working on it."

Grumbling, the boys got up. "What do you feel like doing?" Rodney asked.

Liam knew what he wanted to do. "Let's go see Owen."

When the Driscolls protested that they'd already

been, Liam told them they didn't have to stay. "Just show me where he lives," he said as he got his bike from the garage.

Ten minutes later he coasted into the Bergs' drive-way, waving good-bye as the Driscolls continued on their way. Liam knocked on the front door. A short, stout woman with dark hair piled on top of her head in a messy bun answered. Liam introduced himself and she showed him to the basement rec room. He found Owen and Phillip sitting on a sofa, watching their movie.

"Hey, guys, how are—"

"Shhh!" Owen, eyes glued to the screen, patted the air to hush Liam. "Best part."

Phillip didn't say a word.

Liam stood awkwardly. After a minute he slid into a chair and tried to figure out the movie's plot. Near as he could tell, the story line featured huge explosions, fast car chases, and a deadly robot.

He tried to catch Phillip's eye. But Phillip was appar-ently too engrossed in the action to notice.

Or maybe, a little voice inside Liam said, *he's ignor-ing you.* Liam shifted uncomfortably. The longer Phillip kept his eyes on the screen, the more confused Liam became.

Where was the friendly boy who'd celebrated victory

with him just the day before? He seemed to have vanished. In his place was the pitcher who had given him the cold shoulder for the past weeks.

The scene finally ended with the destruction of the robot. The movie ended there, too. Owen clicked off the television, stretched his arms over the back of the sofa, and acknowledged Liam with a jerk of his head.

Liam asked him how he was feeling.

Owen touched his abdomen gingerly. "Tired of itchy stitches. Bummed I'm out of the game. Happy I'll be in the dugout."

Liam blinked. "In the dugout?"

"Suiting up and sitting with you guys, yeah." He nudged Phillip and grinned. "You and me side by side. Running commentary on the action. Just like old times, huh, DiMadge?"

Phillip flicked a cool gaze at Liam and then smiled at Owen. "You know it, IceBerg." He stood up and moved to the television. "Now how about we plug in the sequel? I've got a feeling that robot isn't really dead."

Owen winged a DVD case to Phillip. "Do it."

"Well," Liam said, "since I missed the first one, I guess I'll be going." He waited a beat to see if either boy would invite him to stay. Neither did. Phillip didn't even turn around from the DVD player. So Liam got up, climbed the stairs, and left. He pedaled for home slowly, mystified and a little hurt by Phillip's behavior.

What happened? Did I do something to make him angry? Is that why he's acting so weird? He racked his brain, turning over everything he'd done or said since the previous day's celebration, but he couldn't come up with an answer. Finally, he gave up.

"Did you find Phillip? Is he coming over today?" Melanie asked when he entered the house.

He shook his head.

She sighed heavily and returned to the computer. "Okay, we'll reschedule the interview. By the way," she added, "Mom called. She says to clean your room because, and I quote, 'if she finds one more open bag of chips under your bed, she's going to take away all your furniture and make you sleep on the bare floor.'" She tossed him a smile over her shoulder.

"Okay," Liam said, only half-listening. He started up to his room, though, to do as his mother asked.

"One more thing," she called after him. "I sent that blooper clip to Carter. Just thought you should know, in case he calls up laughing hysterically."

Liam paused halfway up the stairs. *Carter.*

Last night Phillip had seemed surprised to learn that he and Carter were in touch regularly. Could that possibly be what was bugging him? And if so, why?

Try as he might, he couldn't figure that out. But one thing was for sure: He had to get to the bottom of it, and soon. If not, he could kiss any kind of synchronicity with Phillip good-bye. And if they weren't in sync...

It'll be good-bye, postseason; hello, sidelines.

CHAPTER TWENTY-TWO

Whoa. Look at this place."

Carter and Ash gazed openmouthed at the huge indoor water park spread out before them. Excited screams rang out from each of the six two-story tube slides. An enormous bucket high above a "spray-ground" tipped over and sent a cascade of water onto the delighted people standing below. Low-hanging basketball nets ringed one wading pool. A climbing wall rose above another. Signs pointed the way to hot tubs, a wave pool, and something called a FlowRider.

"Like it?" Mr. Jones said from behind them.

"*Like it?* It's unbelievable!" Carter crowed.

"What do you think, Ashley?" Mrs. LàBrie asked.

"Ash, Mom. *Ash*," her son replied before adding, "Best. Hotel. Ever!"

"Let's go check out our rooms now," Mrs. Jones suggested.

Carter turned away reluctantly. He still couldn't quite believe where he was.

Six hours earlier, when he and Ash had walked in the Joneses' door, Carter nearly stumbled over a suitcase. Other bags, including one with his laptop, were lined up next to it.

He and Ash hurried into the kitchen. "What's with the luggage?" Carter asked.

That's when they learned about the water park hotel. "We're leaving within the hour," Mrs. Jones told him.

"Separate cars, but same hotel," Mrs. LaBrie added. "We're loaded up and ready to go."

Lucky Boy gave a worried bark. "Don't worry, fella," Mr. Jones said. "You'll be staying with Mrs. Flynn next door."

Now Carter turned and said to Ash, "You can't stop me from swimming right away this time, not with three days to spare before the tournament begins!"

"Stop you?" Ash echoed. "Dude, I'll have gone down every slide before you even put on your swimsuit!"

The boys and their parents explored the water park

for the next few hours, stopping only long enough to eat a quick dinner at the park's fast-food restaurant. They returned to their rooms after the park closed, promising to meet up for breakfast the next morning before heading back for more fun.

Carter flopped down on his bed, tired but happy.

Liam would love this place.

The thought jumped unbidden into his brain. He realized he hadn't told Liam where he was going.

Or where you were earlier today, and with who, a little voice inside mocked.

Well, I'll tell him now, he answered the voice defiantly.

He sat up, pulled his laptop from its case, and turned it on. He logged in only to see that Liam was offline. So he decided to send him an e-mail instead. When he opened his account, he saw that he had a message from *mmcgrath,* Melanie's e-mail.

Hey cuz, it read, *thought you'd find this interesting! Enjoy—and good luck at States!*

PS: Don't worry, Liam knows I sent it.

A video file was attached to the e-mail. Curious, he clicked it and then sat back while it downloaded. He wasn't sure what he expected to see, but it sure wasn't what appeared.

Phillip DiMaggio stared out at him from the screen,

his black eyes intense even in the photograph. After a moment, the video began.

Carter watched in fascination as one clip of Phillip after another played. There were dozens of segments of his pitching—waiting for the signal, going through his windup, delivering a pitch. And then, there was one showing his bumping fists three times with Liam.

Carter felt a shock run through his system. He quickly closed the file, shut down the laptop, and got into bed. He refused to think about the fist-bump. Instead, he turned his racing mind to other questions.

Why did Melanie send me that *video? What was in it that she thought I'd find interesting?*

Despite being exhausted from hours in the water park, it took Carter a long time to get to sleep that night. He woke the next morning groggy and out-of-sorts.

"Goodness, you look terrible," his mother said when she saw him. "Are you feeling all right?"

"The boy just needs a good breakfast," Mr. Jones interceded. "Come on. The hotel has some decent choices. Ash and his mom are already there."

Carter did feel a little better once he had something to eat. But he was still thinking about the video. *Maybe if I watch it again,* he thought as he chewed on a bite of waffle, *I'll figure out why she sent it.*

"Hello, earth to Jones! Are you in there, Jones?" Ash waved a hand in front of Carter's face.

Carter blinked. "Huh?"

"I asked if you wanted to look through my binder while I go make a waffle." Ash held out his notebook.

"Yeah, sure." As Carter took the binder, something occurred to him. Ash had a knack for noticing details about players. He was especially tuned in to pitchers. If he watched the video, maybe he'd see whatever Carter had missed.

Ash was silent while the video played, his eyes intently studying Phillip's every move. When the clip was through, he watched it again and then started it for a third time. Midway through that viewing, he gave a sharp cry and paused the film.

"There!" He pointed at Phillip's head. "You see that? He's wiping his face on his arm."

Carter didn't understand why Ash was excited. "So? He does that a lot."

"Exactly! He does it a lot but"—Ash turned to Carter with shining eyes—"only when he's about to throw a changeup. Watch."

He started the video from the beginning. Now that he knew what to look for in those clips, Carter saw it

159

plain as day. First the face-wipe. Then the changeup. Not just once or twice. *Every time.*

"You ever see old movies about the Wild West?" Ash asked. "There's always a scene where a bunch of guys are playing cards. One of them always loses because he has a 'tell,' something like a twitch or a sound that gives away when he's got a good hand. The guy doesn't know he's doing it, but the other players do." He tapped the screen. "We've just discovered Phillip's tell. Now the question is, what do we do with that information?"

"I'll tell you what we do," Carter said. He reached for his cell phone and thumbed to Liam's number. "We warn Liam so he can help Phillip correct it."

Ash snatched the phone from his hands. "You can't be serious!"

"Hey! Give that back!" Carter cried.

Ash held on to the phone. "Look. Before you make the call, just listen to me, will you? First of all, he's probably still asleep."

Carter glanced at the clock and realized Ash was right. It was eight thirty in Pennsylvania, but only five thirty in California. When he nodded, Ash handed back his phone.

"And second," Ash continued, "suppose Forest Park wins States and Regionals and makes it to the World

Series. Suppose Ravenna does, too. Odds are we'd face each other at some point there, right? And maybe Phillip will be on the mound when we do."

Carter understood then what Ash was trying to say. "He's only got two pitches," he said slowly. "The fastball and the changeup. Because of his tell, we'd know which he was going to throw."

Ash nodded. "Imagine what our batters could do if they knew what pitch was coming their way." He leaned in closer. "Maybe that's why Liam let his sister send this. Maybe he's setting a trap for Phillip. Maybe he hopes Phillip will be lit up like a Christmas tree. During the World Series. On national television—and forever on the Internet."

Carter looked at the screen, chewing his bottom lip and considering what Ash suggested. He could see how that would make sense. But was Liam capable of such deviousness?

He didn't think so. But there was only one way to know for sure.

"I'm going to call him. Not now. But before the day is over."

CHAPTER
TWENTY-THREE

IceBerg! You made it!"

The Ravenna players surrounded Owen Berg as if he were a long-lost hero returning from battle. Liam joined in only to have his enthusiastic greeting returned with a cool stare. Phillip gave him the same look before turning to Owen with a huge smile.

Liam retreated and sat down on the bench. He scuffed the sandy dirt beneath his cleats.

There's only one thing I can do, he thought. *If Phillip and I are going to get back in sync, I have to go talk to him and right now. I have to tell him what I've decided.*

But he couldn't seem to make his feet move.

The decision he'd made had come during a phone

call with Carter two days before. He replayed that phone call in his mind now.

His cell phone chirped during breakfast, Carter's number appearing on the screen. He answered after three rings. "Hey, dork, you beat me to it," he said, forcing a jovial tone into his voice. "I was planning to call you later."

"Hey, Liam, listen. I'm calling about the video Melanie sent me."

Carter sounded breathless—from laughing, Liam supposed. "Glad you thought those bloopers of me were so funny," he responded drily.

Silence met his statement. Then he heard whispers and realized someone else was in on the conversation. "Am I on speakerphone?"

"No," Carter replied. "That's just Ash. See, he saw the video, too, and—"

"You know what?" Liam cut in brusquely. He knew he was being rude, but the thought of Ash's watching him behave like an idiot made him flush with embarrassment. "I don't really care what Ash has to say about it. Let's just drop the whole subject of that video, okay?"

"But—"

"Jeez, Carter, I said drop it already!"

Liam heard Carter suck in his breath and immediately regretted his angry outburst. "Listen, I'm sorry."

"No, it's okay. I—you don't want to talk about the video, we won't talk about it." There was a pause, and then Carter asked how things were going in California. "Sean sent a photo of you and Phillip from your last game. Looked like you two were really in sync."

Carter's voice had an edge to it. Liam was going to ask what was wrong but then thought better of it. Carter was a private person who didn't share his troubles easily, not even with Liam. He didn't want to put him on the spot with Ash standing right there.

Ash's presence also kept him from telling Carter why he'd been planning to call him. Liam had arrived at a troubling conclusion. He suspected that his connection with Carter was the reason Phillip was giving him the cold shoulder. The idea had seemed far-fetched until he remembered Phillip's angry reaction to his casual conversations with Sam Witherspoon and the other Malden players. He realized Phillip looked on those players as the enemy. Therefore, he took Liam's friendliness as disloyalty to Ravenna.

If he felt that way about the Malden players, Liam suspected his reaction to his relationship with Carter was one hundred times worse. But what could he do to convince Phillip that Ravenna had his complete allegiance?

There's one solution, he thought. *I could stop talking to Carter for the rest of the season.*

No way was Liam going to suggest that. And yet after his phone call with Carter ended, the idea continued to resurface. Now, in the dugout before the first Sub-Divisional game, he wondered if it wasn't just one solution, but the only solution.

He looked out at Phillip, who was chatting animatedly with Owen. He bit his lip, thinking hard. Then he put his hands on his thighs, pushed up off the bench, and strode over to the pitcher. He planted himself in front of him, hands on hips.

"Phillip, can I talk to you about something?"

Phillip peered up at him. The brim of his cap cast his face in shadow, making it hard for Liam to read his expression.

"This ought to be good," Owen muttered, crossing his arms over his chest and smiling lazily.

Liam ignored him and waited for Phillip's reply.

Phillip stood up. He was taller than Liam, forcing Liam to tilt his head up to maintain eye contact. "What's this about?" he asked, his tone as flinty as his stare.

Liam didn't flinch.

"It's about what happened in the past." He touched his chest, then his nose, and then pointed at Phillip. "And about what's going to happen in the future. In other words: It's about Carter."

Liam and Phillip stared at each other for an endless moment. Then Phillip smiled. "Go ahead. I'm listening."

And with that, Liam started talking.

LITTLE LEAGUE
PERFECT
GAME

MATT CHRISTOPHER

WHAT IS LITTLE LEAGUE®?

With nearly 165,000 teams in all 50 states and over 80 other countries across the globe, Little League Baseball® is the world's largest organized youth sports program! Many of today's Major League players started their baseball careers in Little League Baseball, including Derek Jeter, David Wright, Justin Verlander, and Adrian Gonzalez.

Little League® is a nonprofit organization that works to teach the principles of sportsmanship, fair play, and teamwork. Concentrating on discipline, character, and courage, Little League is focused on more than just developing athletes: It helps to create upstanding citizens.

Carl Stotz established Little League in 1939 in Williamsport, Pennsylvania. The first league only had three teams and played six innings, but by 1946, there were already twelve leagues throughout the state of Pennsylvania. The following year, 1947, was the first year that the Little League Baseball® World Series was played, and it has continued to be played every August since then.

In 1951, Little League Baseball expanded internationally, and the first permanent leagues to form outside of the United States were on either end of the Panama Canal. Little League Baseball later moved to nearby South Williamsport, Pennsylvania, and a second stadium, the Little League Volunteer Stadium, was opened in 2001.

Some key moments in Little League history:

- **1957** The Monterrey, Mexico, team became the first international team to win the World Series.
- **1964** Little League was granted a federal charter.
- **1974** The federal charter was amended to allow girls to join Little League.
- **1982** The Peter J. McGovern Little League Museum opened.
- **1989** Little League introduced the Challenger Division.
- **2001** The World Series expanded from eight to sixteen teams to provide a greater opportunity for children to participate in the World Series.
- **2014** Little League will celebrate its 75th anniversary.

HOW DOES A LITTLE LEAGUE®
TEAM GET TO THE WORLD SERIES?

In order to play in the Little League Baseball® World Series, a player must first be a part of a regular-season Little League, and then be selected as part of their league's All-Star team, consisting of players ages 11 to 13 from any of the teams. The All-Star teams compete in district, sectional, and state tournaments to become their state champions. The state champions then compete to represent one of eight different geographic regions of the United States (New England, Mid-Atlantic, Southeast, Great Lakes, Midwest, Northwest, Southwest, and West). All eight of the Regional Tournament winners play in the Little League Baseball World Series.

The eight International Tournament winners (representing Asia-Pacific, Australia, Canada, the Caribbean, Europe and Africa, Mexico, Japan, and Latin America) also come to the Little League Baseball World Series.

The eight U.S. Regional Tournament winners compete in the United States Bracket of the Little League

Baseball World Series, and the International Tournament winners compete in the International Bracket.

Over eleven days, the Little League Baseball World Series proceeds until a winning U.S. Championship team and International Championship team are determined. The final World Series Championship Game is played between the U.S. Champions and the International Champions.

WANT TO LEARN MORE?

Visit the newly renovated *World of Little League, Peter J. McGovern Museum, and Official Store* in South Williamsport, Pennsylvania! When you visit, you'll find pictures, interactive displays, films, and exhibits showing the history and innovations of Little League.

TEST YOUR LITTLE LEAGUE®
KNOWLEDGE!

1. True or false? The first Little League field, known as Original Little League Field, included an outfield fence.

2. Pennsylvania was the first state to field Little League teams. What was the second?
   a. New York
   b. Connecticut
   c. Virginia
   d. New Jersey

3. Which Baseball Hall of Famer has NOT been a broadcaster at the Little League Baseball® World Series?
   a. Jackie Robinson
   b. Brooks Robinson
   c. Gary Carter
   d. Mickey Mantle

4. How long was the shortest game ever played in Little League Baseball® World Series?
   a. two hours
   b. one hour
   c. thirty minutes
   d. one hour and thirty minutes

5. True or false? Dr. Creighton J. Hale, director of research for Little League in the 1950s and later president of Little League, created the face mask worn by catchers today.

6. In which year did the Little League pitch count rule go into effect?
   a. 1977   c. 1997
   b. 1987   d. 2007

7. True or false? Volunteer Stadium has been in use as long as the Howard J. Lamade Stadium.

8. Where was the first-ever Little League® game played?
   a. Howard J. Lamadé   c. Bowman Field
      Memorial Field   d. Carl Stotz's backyard
   b. Park Point

9. True or false? When Bill Clinton was president of the United States, he hosted a series of Little League Tee Ball games, which were played on the South Lawn of the White House.

10. In 2014, Little League® will be celebrating which milestone anniversary?
   a. silver (25 years)
   b. gold (50 years)
   c. diamond (75 years)
   d. centennial (100 years)

See page 181 for the answers!

HOW CAN I JOIN A LITTLE LEAGUE® TEAM?

If you have access to the Internet, you can see if your community has a local league by going to LittleLeague.org and entering your zip code in the League Finder. You can also visit one of our regional offices:

US REGIONAL OFFICES:
Western Region Headquarters (AK, AZ, CA, HI, ID, MT, NV, OR, UT, WA, and WY)
6707 Little League Drive
San Bernardino, CA 92407
E-MAIL: westregion@LittleLeague.org

Southwestern Region Headquarters (AR, CO, LA, MS, NM, OK, and TX)
3700 South University Parks Drive
Waco, TX 76706
E-MAIL: southwestregion@LittleLeague.org

Central Region Headquarters (IA, IL, IN, KS, KY, MI, MN, MO, ND, NE, OH, SD, and WI)
9802 E. Little League Drive
Indianapolis, IN 46235
E-MAIL: centralregion@LittleLeague.org

Southeastern Region Headquarters (AL, FL, GA, NC, SC, TN, VA, and WV)
PO Box 7557
Warner Robins, GA 31095
E-MAIL: southeastregion@LittleLeague.org

Eastern Region Headquarters (CT, DC, DE, MA, MD, ME, NH, NJ, NY, PA, RI, and VT)
PO Box 2926
Bristol, CT 06011
E-MAIL: eastregion@LittleLeague.org

INTERNATIONAL REGIONAL OFFICES:
CANADIAN REGION (serving all of Canada)
Canadian Little League Headquarters
235 Dale Avenue
Ottawa, ONT
Canada KIG OH6
E-MAIL: Canada@LittleLeague.org

ASIA-PACIFIC REGION (serving all of Asia and Australia)
Asia-Pacific Regional Director
C/O Hong Kong Little League
Room 1005, Sports House
1 Stadium Path
Causeway Bay, Hong Kong
E-MAIL: bhc368@netvigator.com

EUROPE, MIDDLE EAST & AFRICA REGION
(serving all of Europe, the Middle East, and Africa)
Little League Europe
Al. Meleg Legi 1
Kutno, 99-300, Poland
E-MAIL: Europe@LittleLeague.org

LATIN AMERICA REGION (serving Mexico and Latin American regions)
Latin America Little League Headquarters
PO Box 10237
Caparra Heights, Puerto Rico 00922-0237
E-MAIL: LatinAmerica@LittleLeague.org

ANSWERS

1. FALSE!—The outfield fence was erected in 1943, five years after teams began using the field.

2. d—In 1947, Hammerton, New Jersey, founded the first Little League outside of Pennsylvania. In the same year, the first Little League World Series was played.

3. c—Jackie Robinson, Brooks Robinson, and Mickey Mantle have each attended the Little League Baseball® World Series as guest commentators for the radio or television coverage of the tournament. Gary Carter has also visited the World Series, but not as a broadcaster.

4. b—In 1950, eight teams participated in the Little League Baseball® World Series. Kankakee, Illinois, and Hagerstown, Maryland, were both defeated in the semifinals. They played each other in a consolation game that lasted exactly one hour. Illinois won 1–0.

5. FALSE!—Dr. Creighton J. Hale, namesake of the Creighton J. Hale International Grove, created the protective batting helmet, not the face mask, in 1959.

6. d—In 2007, Little League International implemented the first official pitch count rule, aimed at protecting young pitchers' arms from injury caused by repetitive motion and overuse. The rule was put into effect following extensive medical research.

7. FALSE!—Construction on Volunteer Stadium began in 2000, in anticipation of the Little League Baseball World Series expansion from eight to sixteen teams in 2001. Construction was completed in time for the tournament. Lamade Stadium was built in 1959.

8. b—The first organized Little League® baseball game was played on June 6, 1939, at Park Point in Williamsport, PA. The plot of ground where the game was played is located beyond the centerfield fence at Historic Bowman Field, a minor league baseball stadium in Williamsport.

The first game was a 23–8 win for Lundy Lumber over Lycoming Dairy.

9. FALSE!—Tee Ball games were played on the South Lawn of the White House, but it was baseball lover, Little League supporter, and former U.S. president George W. Bush who organized the initiative. The first games were played in 2001.

10. c—Little League was founded in 1939, making 2014 the 75th anniversary season for the program founded in Williamsport, PA, by Carl E. Stotz.